What Goes Around

What Goes Around

David O'Neal

David O'Neal (signature)

A Pacific Coast Press publication

What Goes Around
A Pacific Coast Press publication, March 1998

This is a work of fiction. All characters, incidents, dialogue, names and plots are creations of the author's imagination. Any similarity to actual persons living or dead, companies or events is unintended and purely coincidental.

If you bought this book without a cover, you should be aware that you have purchased stolen property. A retailer reported to the publisher that this book was unsold and thus destroyed. Neither the author nor the publisher received any payment for such stripped books.

ISBN 0-9660851-0-8

First Edition

Pacific Coast Press, PO Box 26857, San Jose, CA 95159

* The photo image for the cover art was obtained from IMSI's Master Photos Collection, 1895 Francisco Blvd. East, San Rafael, CA 94901-5506, USA.

To my friends and family who gave so unselfishly,
you know who you are.
Thanks for making my vision a reality.

"All systems maintain their own equilibrium. Change imposes stress (divergence) and highly stressed systems are said to be in disequilibrium. Somehow that logic seems faulty to me.

"Divergence doesn't bring disequilibrium because disequilibrium can not exist like that. Actually systems shift to a new seemingly arbitrary balance point and people are unhappy living within that particular state of the system."

Doug Carlson

Chapter One

In crowded casinos the late nights are considered early. Doug moved unconsciously to avoid brushing a player next to him. Using weary fingers he clasped his hands behind the stool. With a strong grip he flexed the muscles of both arms to relieve a growing fatigue. He breathed softly. Recirculated air filled his six-foot frame.

Blackjack dealers make their jobs look easy, he mused through a faint smile of delight. Most handle their cards with accurate, efficient snaps, then with a quick peek play as if assured of a winning outcome.

Months ago Doug had decided that Sammy's dealing was no exception to that observation. Playing at her table most of the evening, he had won several thousand dollars but she had made much more for the casino.

As Sammy shuffled a new deck, Doug decided to play one last hand. He anted three one-hundred-dollar chips. The cut was offered ritualistically to the chain-smoking woman at the other end of the table. Doug watched their interaction and sighed. Sleep was closing in fast.

The last few days had been enjoyable and profitable for him, a nice welcome change. Too often he experienced only drunkenness followed by boredom and he was trying to mend those uncomfortable behaviors.

The first card arrived as he gulped the last of his warm beer. He paused briefly with the bottle. Reducing his alcohol intake to one-bottle an hour was probably why he had won more money during this trip.

His second card arrived face-up. It was an Eight.

He peeked at the down card, an Ace, probably a winner.

Sammy's card was a Six.

Doug leaned into the heavily padded stool. He brushed strong, skillful fingers through shortly cropped blond hair as he thought about his game strategy.

He decided to risk losing the hand in order to double the payoff on his bet.

The young man sitting to his right took a hit and busted with 25. Without hesitating Sammy was ready for Doug.

Their gaze locked for an instant. Staring into her focused eyes, he flipped the Ace face-up on the green felt.

"Double-down, please."

Sammy dealt a single card facedown on the table and continued to the next player.

Doug watched the play move past him and toward the dealer. Bust. Hold. Bust.

Sammy turned over a One-Eyed-Jack for herself. The house has 16, he thought. After a brief pause she dealt the mandatory hit, a Seven of Hearts.

The house had busted.

Sammy looked up and focused on Doug as she reached for a stack of chips to pay his wager.

He flipped his unseen card, knowing that he would win with anything. It was a three.

The older gentleman to Doug's left was excited and patted him several times on the back.

"Son, you've got the best dog-gone luck I've ever seen! You just beat the house with a twelve. That's excellent."

The man broke into laughter.

Sammy smiled at the scene as she paid Doug's winnings from a stack of one-hundred-dollar chips.

Doug rose and pushed a hundred-dollar chip across the table. He smiled as Sammy picked it up, tapped the table and put it with her tips.

"Well, Sammy, I've had enough fun for one night." He looked straight into her blue eyes. "It's been a pleasure as usual. I'll see you on my next trip."

Through a brief glance she smiled and nodded. "Thanks, see you then, Doug. Have a safe drive back to Los Angeles."

A jumble of party sounds from the casino's activity filled Doug's ears as he walked away and headed for a nearby cage to redeem the chips bulging in three of his pockets. Nearing the cashier he intercepted a bar hostess and took someone else's cold beer for a ten-dollar tip.

After converting the chips he lingered at several game tables, enjoying the atmosphere. He sipped on the bottle of beer. The odor of cigarette smoke filled the air.

Through a background of soft chamber music he heard the endless plinking of slot-machine coins. There was the occasional blast of excitement when someone hit a jackpot.

Doug passed the bay of slot machines where he had played earlier in the day. Feeding the slots had been fun, especially the progressive-dollar machines but playing Blackjack was his favorite. He paused to watch an elderly couple feed quarters into a slot machine and smiled at their delight when a fifty-dollar jackpot arrived.

Doug gulped the remaining beer and strolled into the Fountain Room for a nightcap. He scoped out the dimly lit lounge and found a seat at the far end of the bar.

He ordered a Metoxa boilermaker and paid the bartender ten-dollars for the four-dollar drink, downed the shot then turned-up the glass of beer and gulped a quarter of it.

This would be his last drink.

Gazing around the dimly lit room, he settled into the soft bar stool to enjoy the piano vocalist. He thought about how gratifying the last few days had been but recalled that not all of his friends would agree.

Several expressed concerns about Las Vegas' around-the-clock-pace, claiming it was too risky for law-abiding people like him. Although he listened to well-meaning complaints, none seemed valid in light of his personal experiences.

So far, he had been fortunate to meet only nice, friendly people with the best of intentions. Since he had been escaping to Las Vegas, he had never met anyone to change his mind. He liked the unrestrained festivities and for now that was what mattered most to him.

He left the bar with a half-empty glass of beer to pickup his room key. He took a small sip.

It was a treat for Doug to stroll through the luxury of a lavishly decorated casino, hotel and lobby. He had certainly enjoyed his stay at The Golden Phoenix.

As he entered the lobby, Doug saw a crowd mingling around the Registration Desk. The din of arriving tourists filled the air. Their presence obscured the main entrance.

He maneuvered without incident around several bystanders but as he neared the end of a long line, a huge man turned without warning and bumped into him.

The impact was hard and the partially full glass slipped from his fingers, hit another person's arm and rolled across the floor. The remaining beer spilled on the front of the mammoth's clothing.

The collision startled Doug and he gasped. "Oh! Excuse me, sir. I'm very sorry."

The well dressed, heavyset man had already lost his temper. Through a thick Brooklyn accent his voice boomed.

"Hey, look what you've done!" Then he motioned with beefy palms. "Ah, . . . look at that! You've even gone and soiled my pants and shoes."

Several of the man's friends had already passed but hesitated, returned and crowded menacingly around Doug.

"Hold on!" Doug protested. "I already said it was my fault and I'm really sorry but don't worry. I'll gladly pay for the damage."

Doug reached for his wallet to give the man a twenty.

"Here . . .."

One of the man's friends pushed through the crowd. He was tall and skinny but acted like he weighed an extra hundred pounds. His outstretched hand reached for Doug like he was ready to fight with him.

With the same kind of accent he spoke. "Mr. C, let me take care of this creep for you."

With a slight hand gesture, the big man restrained him.

"That's okay, Mario. I can handle this bum."

In an elevated voice he continued the tirade. "Why don't you watch where you're going? You know, people get hurt real bad for doing less than what you just got away with."

Several guests stopped to watch but Mario chased them away with verbal insults.

Stepping backwards, Doug glanced around the room for help but few others noticed.

With his wallet in one hand Doug raised his palms toward Mr. C. "Look, Mister, I said I was sorry. I don't want any trouble with you or your pals. Just let me give you some cash and I'm out of here."

In a fist fight Doug could handle three men. The Marine Corps had taught him that many years ago. As a civilian he learned that tact was less painful.

Trying to maintain control, Doug hoped to end the confrontation without a fight or any more hard feelings but it was not happening that way.

The other men moved closer to Mario and no longer encircled Doug.

Mr. C's face turned red as his anger boiled-over but his voice softened. "What are you trying to do now, insult me again with your lousy money? Get out of my face, you bum, before you really make me mad."

Doug realized the situation could get out of control and escalate. He offered one last apology trying to sound sincere. "I'm really sorry, Mister." Then turned and walked away.

Hesitating a moment, Mr. C's group walked away too. After less than a dozen steps, Mr. C turned to Mario.

"Find out where that guy's staying," he whispered. "I'm not done with him yet! Then meet us in the Fountain Room."

The beanpole of a man responded. "No problem, Mr. C. I'll get that for you and be right there."

Doug unlocked the door to his room and pushed it open. The maid had been there during the day. The room was clean and neat, just as he expected it to be.

Tossing the room key on the bar, he kicked off his shoes and took a bottle of ice-cold fruit juice from the small fridge. He twisted off the bottle cap and took a long cold drink. Its sweet taste contrasted with all the beer he had drunk that day. He hung his navy-blue jacket on a chair and sat to relax.

He yawned as he opened a schedule of upcoming Las Vegas events. Glancing through the pages, he found several shows he would enjoy.

It would be nice to stay longer but he could not take any more time-off from his job for a while.

Closing the magazine, he took another sip then moved to a softer chair to recline and stretch out his legs.

The clock radio beamed 11:48 p.m. Doug was tired and ready for bed. Another yawn came without his noticing.

He took out his wallet and counted the handful of bills. This would be one of the few times he would go home with extra cash. He finished the last of his drink and set the empty bottle on the bar.

Yawning again, he disrobed and headed for the shower.

Mario listened with his ear to the door while Gino picked the lock. The room was quiet. A third man, Lenny, stood at the end of the corridor, prepared to divert approaching guests. No one had seen them yet.

After a minute of futile resistance the lock responded and the door opened with a click.

Using hand signals, the men moved silently into the room. Mario clutched a .38 revolver in his right hand but neither of the other men carried guns.

The room was well lit but no one was in sight.

An empty bottle sat on the bar next to a numbered room key. A pile of discarded men's clothing was tossed carelessly across the end of a turned-down bed.

"Are you sure he was in room 1044?" Lenny whispered.

Mario responded with his usual degrading manner. "Of course, you idiot, that's the room number he asked for." In disgust Mario made a gesture in Lenny's direction.

Lenny checked out the balcony but found no one. Gino listened for sounds at a door by the bar and upon opening it discovered a walk-in closet.

Mario moved quietly around the room, inspecting everything. Finally he stopped to listen at the bathroom door.

He heard running water. Mario turned the knob slowly and peeked inside. Steam bellowed through the crack.

A man was taking a shower.

Mario stepped back and motioned for the other men to come closer. He placed a finger to his lips. "Shhhh."

In a moment the men stood silently outside the door. The intruders waited like ravenous tigers for the right moment to pounce. A few seconds later the water stopped.

A muscular arm reached outside the shower for a towel.

Doug stepped carefully out of the tub to a bath mat. He dried himself without noticing the door was ajar.

Holding the towel over his head, he vigorously dried his face, head and hair. When the towel obscured his eyes, the goons seized the opportunity.

Mario kicked the door and its brass knob thundered into the glazed tile of the adjoining wall.

Doug jerked in surprise and slipped to the floor. Catching his breath, he recognized Mario standing in the doorway holding a gun.

Before Doug could speak, Mario stepped forward and planted a powerful kick into the middle of his chest. The impact threw Doug backward into the side of the tub.

Pain flared in his chest, shoulders and head. The other men rushed forward to grab him but Doug went limp.

Gino swore and kicked the back of Doug's exposed thigh. The clumsily aimed boot slid along Doug's inner thigh ending in his groin.

Mario intervened. "Okay, guys, just pick him up! It's time for a man-to-man talk."

Gino and Lenny grabbed Doug's arms. Squeezing tightly, they lifted him off the floor.

Unaware of what was happening Doug managed to stand

on wobbly legs.

"Mr. C don't like your kind asshole!" Mario taunted as he moved into Doug's face. "And he especially don't like you. Your rude shit downstairs just don't cut it, understand?"

Doug tried to speak. He moved his lips but nothing came through a prolonged grimace.

"So, . . . I handle the jerks like you."

Mario glanced proudly between his accomplices.

With a big smile he closed in on Doug again. He growled menacingly. "I think I'll just shoot your ass. What do you think about that?"

Doug knew he had to speak and after a moment managed to utter only a muffled moan.

Mario leaned closer, turned his head slightly and whispered. "What was that, punk? Did you say something? I couldn't quite hear it."

Doug struggled to stand.

He was ready to start throwing punches. He shifted his weight, flexed his arms and tried to loosen their grip but his captors held even tighter.

Adrenaline started pumping as he paused, then spoke in a quivering, pained voice. "What's this all about?"

"I told you. We don't like you, jerk-off. You got a problem with that?" Mario raised the gun to make his point and rested it on the tip of Doug's nose.

Doug knew he was in deep doodoo. His heart pounded. Standing straighter, he responded. "Well, . . ."

Mario withdrew the gun several inches.

Ready to strike at Mario, Doug squirmed to detect weakness in his captor's grip. There was none. He would not be able to break free.

Defiantly he continued. " . . . then up your . . .."

Mario's response was as quick as his temper. With a thud the gun slammed into the side of Doug's head. Both men released their grip and he slid into a broken pile.

"That'll teach you, . . . what a dumb-ass fucker!" Mario shouted in disgust.

Returning to the bedroom Gino grabbed for Doug's pants and quickly rifled them.

Finding a wallet, he spoke through a big grin. "We might as well make this trip a little sweeter. Hey Mario, look at the cash this guy has. He's loaded! Looks like a couple a grand. What'a you think, Mario?"

Mario moved closer as the count began.

"Whoa, this guy's got $3,800 and change."

"Okay, give me two grand. You guys split what's left."

Gino counted four five-hundred-dollar bills and handed them to Mario. He jammed the rest into his rear pocket.

The other man jumped at him. "Hey, half that's mine."

"Don't worry about it, Lenny! You'll get yours but let's get the fuck out of here first." He replaced the wallet and carelessly tossed the pants across the bed.

Mario gave the final orders. "Okay, we'll meet Mr. C downstairs in ten minutes." Each man left Doug's room in a different direction.

Several hours later Doug awakened.

The cold of the bathroom floor chilled his skin. The damp towel over his right foot provided his only warmth. His head throbbed.

With partially open eyes he squinted in pain at the glare from the overhead lights. His eyes watered. Tears streamed into his ears.

Eventually he focused on the ceiling and then on the corner of the wall. He was still alive but did not feel much like it. His head ached. It hurt to even open his eyes so he closed them just for the momentary rush of relief.

His attention was seized by a dull ache in the middle of his stomach. A feeling difficult for most men to mistake for anything else, one of those goons had kicked him squarely in the balls. He knew from past experience the throb would subside in a few hours.

Lying on the bathroom floor, Doug flexed his hands, arms and legs, testing each for pain and injury. Each felt fine except for his right thigh, which was sore from the kick. Somewhere in his pounding head, he remembered that if you could move a body part then it was not broken.

Holding onto the bathtub for support, he sat up.

Grasping the tub again, he lifted himself slowly, trying to stand. Halfway up, he reached for the edge of the counter. Persisting, he rose to an awkward standing position, watching himself in the mirror. His mature, pleasant looking face grimaced in pain. The side of his head was bruised from his eye to a numb left ear.

Fumbling for aspirin among his toiletries, he took four.

Turning on the cold water, he splashed it across his face. The refreshing feeling brought little relief for the pain in his head. He took a long drink of water and sat on the toilet seat.

As the throbbing continued, he picked up the damp towel. Covering his shoulders, he leaned against the wall and closed his eyes.

Doug was awakened at nine o'clock the next morning. During the night, he felt chilled and stumbled into bed without remembering it. He pulled the blankets around his neck and slept dreamlessly until the wake-up call arrived.

The alert voice on the telephone caused Doug to sit-up in bed with a jerk. He still had the crushing headache but he thanked the caller and hung-up the receiver.

His head fell back onto the pillows and he stared reflectively at the ceiling as he remembered the events from the prior night. He recalled the names, Mario and Mr. C. He wondered who those people were and what caused that situation to get so out of control.

His awareness sought the secret places of a man's mind where he felt safe. In an instant he had an answer. For some men the only solution to a problem was beating the shit out of anyone who got in their way.

That brief insight made his situation quite simple. He had spilled a drink on Mr. C so Mario had settled the score. According to male myth, that was how it worked. In Mr. C's eyes they were even. That would probably be the end of it.

Doug's thoughts became jumbled as they drifted among distant memories. In the past when things around him were uncertain like this he pretended they were fine. That pretense made them easier. That was how he maintained his sanity. He prepared to let go of this incident the same way.

His head throbbed so he limped toward the bathroom for more aspirins. He took two with a sip of water.

During the next twenty minutes he showered and dried himself. He found a bruise on his chest, one on the back of his thigh and one on his face to the left of his eye.

His head still hurt but now it was tolerable.

He called the front desk for a porter to pick up his bags in a half-hour so they would be available for him when he checked out. He finished dressing, packed his luggage and went downstairs to The Windjammer Cafe for breakfast.

Twenty-five minutes later, Doug reached into his wallet for a ten-dollar bill to pay for the meal but the cash pocket was empty. He searched its other pockets.

His cash was gone.

In a whisper he cursed. "God damn you, Mario. You're a fucking thief! After what you did to me, why would you rob me too? You're a rotten sleaze-bag, motherfucker."

Doug noticed his voice had escalated as others turned to look at him. He felt a blush cover his cheeks.

Gaining his composure, he smiled through embarrassment at a young couple. Another irritated onlooker shook his head in disgust, then continued with his meal.

Instead of cash Doug tossed a credit card onto the tray with his breakfast bill. The waitress returned with the charge slip as he swallowed his final bite of an English muffin and gulped the last of his chilled tomato juice.

Seeing Doug prepare to leave the waitress approached to clear the table and pickup the charge slip.

He returned her smile and walked out of the café toward the checkout desk. In the distance Doug heard the sounds of fun from the casino. He fought the urge to drop a few coins and strolled in the opposite direction.

Walking up to the empty counter, he said. "Check me out of room 1044, please."

"I'll be right with you, sir." A young woman answered. The name on her badge identified her as the manager.

Doug had not seen her there before. Waiting, he turned, looking casually around the lobby while she finished.

There was surprisingly little activity in sight around him. Near the entrance a porter assisted a silver-haired couple by pushing their luggage toward the desk. Two young black porters stood chatting several feet to his left at the end of the counter. A lone woman sat in a stuffed chair to the right of a picturesque sofa, preparing colorful postcards to be mailed.

At 10:30 in the morning, Doug expected to see more guests in the lobby.

As the manager's attention returned to Doug, she asked. "Sir, that was room 1044?"

Feeling interrupted, he turned toward her but responded politely. "Yes, that's right."

Thumbing through a file, she located his paperwork before speaking. "Let's see . . . here it is. Shall I put this on your credit card, Mr. Carlson?"

She paused, waiting for him to respond.

"Sure."

Several seconds later Doug asked. "Excuse me, Miss. I called earlier to have my luggage picked-up. Is it here, yet?"

The woman spoke to one of the nearby porters. "Joey, did you pick up the bags in 1044?"

Joey jumped, pointing toward the front door. "There, that cart near the entrance." He moved closer.

The second porter shifted his position leaning forward a bit but still resting his elbows on the counter. His attention focused on Doug.

Holding out a hand, Joey approached. "Can I bring your car around, sir?"

Doug tossed three keys on a key ring to him. "Okay. It's a red Mustang. Put the top down if you don't mind, Joey."

Turning toward the manager, Doug asked. "I need some cash for the road. Please add an extra fifty dollars to my bill if you don't mind, Miss."

"Sure, it'll take just a moment, Mr. Carlson."

As the manager worked, Doug asked. "I ran into an interesting gentleman here last night. One of his friends called him Mr. C. Do you happen to know who he was?"

Puzzled, she looked up and responded while shaking her

head. "No, I don't think I've heard that name before but then I only started working here three weeks ago"

"Well I just thought I'd ask. Maybe I'll see him here another time." Doug signed the charge slip, stuck forty-five dollars in his wallet and put the other five into his shirt pocket. It was a tip for Joey.

He walked away from the counter.

The manager barked at the remaining porter. "Look alive, Ralph! Help Mr. Carlson with his bags."

As Doug neared the entrance Ralph had already rushed ahead of him to get the cart. "I'll get that for you, sir."

Doug nodded and continued walking through the entrance to where his car should have been waiting.

Behind him, he heard Ralph pushing the luggage cart. "Looks like that doorknob got the best of you, friend!"

Doug did not respond.

"Was it Mr. C who done that to you? If you ask me he's a bad motherfucker but I guess you already learned that, huh? You're pretty lucky, Mister. You know, not to be dead and being wheeled out on a cart too. Of course around here people just disappear in the desert."

Doug stopped. "You know that guy?"

"Well not exactly but I've heard about what he's done to other guys who got in his way like you did."

"But do you know his name?"

"Sure. His name is Dante Frederico de Casale. A hell of a good sounding name for such a bad dude, huh? Sounds like he ought to be a Duke or some kind of royalty, don't it?

"He comes in here every month, always on the second weekend just like clockwork. Weird if you ask me. He and his guys probably go through 'bout a hundred babes or so. It must cost a fortune if you ask me . . . .."

Doug chuckled.

Ralph sounded like a babbling chipmunk.

Halting his laughter, Doug asked. "Ralph, don't you ever shut up? I only asked the guy's name."

Ralph laughed but continued as if nothing had been said.

"Oh, yeah! Well his boys usually call him Mr. C but his business associates call him Fred. Yeah, Fred. Can you believe that? Just like he's a regular guy but I know he ain't. He's one mean, fucking, bad dude! He doesn't let anyone get in his way or interrupt his party time. What'd you do to get him so pissed at you?"

Doug looked for his car. It should have arrived by then.

Ralph repeated his question so Doug answered just to shut him up. "I accidentally spilled some beer on him last night, okay."

Ralph could not hide his surprise.

"Say, where's your pal, Joey?"

"Whoa, Dude! You're lucky he didn't plant you in some skuzzy, rat infested warehouse dumpster across town. From the looks of your eye, he let you off easy. He must like you, I'd say. You know . . .."

Doug's impatience began to grow. "Ralph, where in hell is your pal, Joey?"

"Oh, uh . . . well, Joey sort of gets carried away sometimes, test driving the nice wheels he brings up but it's usually only for a few blocks. For him to be gone this long means you got a fine 'shine, Bro. I remember once . . .."

Suddenly, Joey and Doug's car appeared, sliding around the corner to the left. The top was down, tires squealed and heads turned.

Even Ralph stopped speaking in mid-sentence but not for long. "Oh, I think that's him now."

Ralph's understatement was clear and everybody within hearing distance knew it. He added. "Nice wheels!"

Joey stopped the car directly in front of them without a sound. He got out and beamed a grin across the top of the car looking like a five-year-old with a brand-new toy.

"I gassed her up for you, Mister. The tank's full of premium. Oil and water checks okay. You're all set for the road, my man! It cost fourteen and change."

He stepped away from the car, left the engine running and the door open.

Doug was unsure whether to be upset or praise the kid but what Joey had done was nice. After pausing he decided to let it go. After all Joey had done him a favor and saved him some time so he went along with the situation.

"So how's she handle in the turns, Joey?" Grabbing his wallet, Doug took out a twenty and folded it for Joey.

"Ah man. You got a hot, finely tuned road machine, Bro. Mustang has been fine 'bout forever. You even listen to *rad* tunes, my man!"

Joey did a little shuffle, demonstrating his pleasure as he stepped away from the door.

Doug walked around the car and handed the bill to Joey. Then he turned toward Ralph and motioned for him to move closer. He did.

"Thanks, for telling me about Fred. You're a good man." Doug handed him the five-dollar bill from his shirt pocket, slid into the driver's seat and closed the door.

Ralph leaned over, putting his hands on the door.

"Listen," he said in a soft serious tone.

"I've heard Fred's with the Mafia some kind of a boss or something like that but I don't know the details. They say he kills people just for fun and does it on a regular basis.

"You really are lucky to be alive, Mister so be careful next time you're around him."

Joey moved beside Ralph, nodding.

Doug glanced toward the exit and both men stepped back a few steps. "Thanks, fellows, see ya 'round."

The Mustang inched forward. Each mumbled a farewell.

Doug drove west, then turned onto Highway 15. It would be a long trip back to his home in Los Angeles.

Chapter Two

Doug relaxed as he drove the open road. Light traffic required so little effort. Driving in the proper lane and keeping the speed under 80 were its only demands. This made life more enjoyable; it was easy and simple.

When relaxed, his mind drifted through nearly forgotten memories. He marveled at how easily his cares faded during such moments. Sheltered havens filled his mind with uninterrupted contemplation and self-examination.

During the last few hours his mind had processed a flurry of recollections and explored a variety of seemingly unrelated mind images. He felt relaxed by them.

Green eyes bathed with age. Doug's pounds flowed over an agile frame; only regular jogging and a daily sit-up routine kept them under control. He was strong and fit.

Confidence filled him. Although not usually arrogant he was capable of narcissistic feelings, thoughts and occasional escapes into daydreaming and fantasy.

Mostly the past weekend was fun and relaxing. It started last Thursday evening when he left his home in Venice. The highway was mostly deserted during the seven-hour drive. He arrived at the casino just in time for an early breakfast.

As usual, Doug scoped-out the casino for the first few hours, looking for familiar faces and making new friends. He chatted with several people including two attractive women.

Both were young, outgoing and available but neither had

that sense of emotional togetherness that was now more important to him.

Catherine had it but she could not join him on this trip.

At forty-one, Doug was satisfied with relationships that offered emotional potential rather than surface glitz. Sex was easy to find these days, especially in Las Vegas but it was also quite easy for him to pass it up.

Doug held no illusions that meaningful relationships and lasting friendships were difficult to find. They were just as hard to nurture and maintain. They required a unique kind of sharing, a form of intimacy that many of his friends had not yet learned to even discuss.

For him a person's ultimate success in life also required a mature willingness to disagree. After all, nobody including him ever really wanted things done only their way.

Life experience had taught Doug that most stereotypes were false. He expressed to his friends that using clichés to describe life regularly deprived them of the opportunity to make useful decisions.

As the years passed, Doug's life grew harder instead of easier. While he made friends with most he met, his upsets involved only his own changing expectations.

His boyhood habits of being, thinking and interacting were not what he chose for himself today. Once he began doing things differently, it dawned on him that most people rarely kept friends who routinely failed to agree with them.

A seldom-exposed feeling was that society might evolve and become better than it had been. That was what he really wanted. He had actually dreamed of ways to make it happen.

Being more focused on the future than the past, he sought to understand the politics and issues of the day. Disturbingly he concluded that quite different solutions were possible than those reported in the media and from those of many of his friends. This was Doug's biggest annoyance. Society's generally bad attitude about managing itself.

Doug stopped around 3:30 for lunch at a musty roadside diner. A small, colorless building, old and run-down but visually tolerable, located somewhere outside Victorville.

The food was okay and filling. After his meal he relaxed while drinking half of a second bottle of beer before getting back on the road.

Most of the day he had driven in a southwesterly direction. Now the sun was low in the western sky.

Billowing, fluffy clouds hung like fresh laundry in the distance. They added a lot to a sunset if they did not block it completely. This would be a good one to stop and watch.

Ten miles later Doug pulled off the highway. He parked on an old nearly forgotten side road, put up the top and turned off the engine. He grabbed a jacket from the trunk and leaned against the grill to watch the sun disappear.

A stiff breeze made the night air especially cold. He slipped frosty hands into cozy pockets. In December the desert at dusk was chilly.

The vivid colors and allure of the sunset has been special for Doug since he was eight years old. He could tell this one would be breathtaking.

As a child, he remembered sitting on the steps of his front porch, watching the sun slip behind mountains far in the distance. Those brief moments of silence helped him recall and later organize the daily happenings that eventually shaped his life. Even then, he knew life could be much better than it actually was.

Doug left home immediately after high school but close family ties tugged painfully for him to return. He was driven by something more intense, yet still hidden.

He joined the Marines to get away from home and fully experience a budding ego. Little did he know at the time how well it would work.

The Marines trained him as a weapons specialist and like most men growing up in the sixties, he headed immediately to Vietnam. After his third combat operation, he was recommended for a Silver Star Medal. Instead he got a Purple Heart that sent him home after nine months to recover from a bullet in the butt.

Doug praised the Marines because they taught him motivation, self-respect and personal discipline. Vietnam taught him pain, despair and his own sense of humanity. Strangely, he continued to love them both.

After his shortened tour of duty, Doug completed college, then graduate school. Those early years were the most difficult because he felt so alone even in a crowd.

Although a seeker at heart Doug sought a down-to-earth attitude. Disappointment gripped him when he failed to find ways of merging his idealism with his realism. He strongly defended his beliefs sometimes to the point of disregarding everything else around him.

Most issues were easily sorted. The things of interest to him that he defended and cared about because they adversely affected him and the things he disregarded because he did not care about then or they did not bother him.

Doug shivered from the intense cold. His light jacket now offered little comfort. With hands and arms now folded over his chest he shook uncontrollably from head to toe.

The sun was gone and he had become so completely absorbed in the sunset that he failed to notice the cold.

This was how sunsets affected Doug. His thoughts took on a life of their own. He easily got lost in recollections or contemplation sometimes for hours.

Trying to remember where he had lost track of the sunset, Doug recalled getting tattooed.

He had been a Jarhead for a year. Enormous pride filled him and he wanted to broadcast it. Joined by several leatherneck buddies, he visited a little parlor near the beach in San Clemente where he had the Eagle, Globe and Anchor tattooed on his right arm near the shoulder.

Many others in his squad also did the same. Everyone agreed it could be easy to lose your dog tags in battle but you were less likely to lose an arm. It was a bit of extra insurance against becoming the next Unknown Soldier.

Climbing behind the wheel, he started the engine and sat, waiting for warm air to flow. He had parked on a narrow side road a hundred feet off the main highway.

At home this would have been a dangerous place to stop. Without streetlights too many shadows hid those who would sneak-up without warning.

It's outrageous! Too few city streets are safe; too many tax dollars are spent on the police, jails and prisons for them to still be so deadly. Something's seriously wrong and nobody's able to understand the problem, much less develop ideas or plans to fix them.

When heat arrived, he drove toward the highway. As he approached the on-ramp, he noticed no other cars in sight.

The light traffic offered less chance for another drivers' mistakes to affect him. He accepted many risks but that was an unnecessary one.

Smiling at the situation, he hoped it stayed that way. He would make good time during the rest of the trip.

He turned right toward San Bernardino as his reflection on society's deterioration continued.

People seem to worry less about personal safety today

than they did twenty years ago. Sure, there were fewer peo-
ple in those days and most had jobs to keep them busy; those
without jobs had families to take care of them. Welfare was
handled better in those days than it is today.

Doug did not understand why people talked about out-of-control-crime as if it magically appeared last month. To him there was no current crime problem, only failed solutions.

He claimed to know of only two types of crime. Those committed by the *needy* and those carried-out by the *greedy*. Now even those distinctions fade. Both appear to be rampant and equally destructive in rich societies.

The wisdom of having a gun nearby occurred to him. Did it make a person feel safer? That was not the case for him.

He had a pistol but could not remember ever using it. He bought it shortly after the Marines but he had not seen or handled it for many years.

In a weird sort of way he felt safer ten years ago.

The pistol might have helped create that feeling but who knows, maybe there was less crime then. He did not have an answer. Certainly there seemed to be more of it today.

Maybe he would feel safer if he located the gun and kept it handy. It might have been useful this weekend.

He knew that crime was not really the problem since commonplace weirdness had become the norm. It occurred everywhere one looked. It was the central focus of some people's everyday behavior. They were proud of the individuality it brought them. The ones who fell straight to earth from the twilight zone were proud to explore and nurture it.

Today, it seemed that few could live or have fun without it being at someone else's expense. They ridiculed different ideas or behavior as if it was meaningful debate.

To Doug it was all so simple--such people took themselves and their feelings much too seriously and those running the country failed to acknowledge it as a problem.

Doing the right thing was no longer respectable. The simple courtesies were gone. Doug remembered when an accidental bump produced apologies from both parties who then went about their business.

In many of today's cities such actions produced a barrage of mindless insults. In the others one could expect a fight or a drive-by-shooting to happen later in the evening.

It seems that the biggest, the strongest and the most powerful often have special rules that apply only to them and help maintain their unique, often superior status. When they accumulate enough thugs, weapons, money or power, then effectively they can place themselves above the law and thus untouchable by it.

Doug was sure that Mr. C always had a handful of goons at his side to deal with such discourtesies. That way, he kept himself clean and respectable. Doug guessed that Mr. C was a perfectly law-abiding man in his own neighborhood.

There seemed to be little room for debate. With the exertion of enough personal force one could be safe. That was probably all that mattered to such people: bigger police forces, larger security staffs or more bodyguards.

Somehow the obligation to be responsible for one's own behavior and its consequences was no longer respectable.

If the law of the jungle ever prevailed, these characters would be threatened just like the masses, primarily because there would always be somebody bigger, stronger, richer or more powerful.

In times like that, right or wrong would not matter, only the destructive force one could apply to the situation.

Like a bolt of lightning streaking across a darkened sky, Doug's attention jolted back to the road.

In the darkness ahead he saw another car. His car traveled at more than 90 miles per hour. *That's much too fast.*

He eased off the accelerator and the speed fell toward 80.

Closing the gap, he saw two cars instead of one. As his speed fell, he watched the distance between them narrow.

Doug passed both cars doing 70 miles per hour. They looked new, dark in color and expensive. One was a limo. They drove at the posted speed limit.

Mr. C napped periodically but now he was awake, relaxing in the back seat of the black limo. Three bodyguards traveled in the blue Town Car ahead of him.

He glimpsed the speeding Mustang and was sure he recognized the driver. "Hey, Mario, wasn't that the clown who spilled beer on my suit yesterday?"

Mario glanced out the window but was too late to see the driver's face. He picked up the car phone.

"I couldn't tell Mr. C but I'll call ahead to the guys. Maybe they'll get a better look at him."

He pressed a speed-dial button on the telephone and in a moment began speaking. "Hey, Gino. Check out that car coming up behind you."

"Yeah."

"Mr. C thinks it's the guy from the casino. Remember, the one in room 1044?"

"You know," Gino responded. "it looks a little like him! Hold on. I'll see what Lenny says."

The telephone went silent for a moment.

"Yeah, Mario. Tell Mr. C that we think it's him too."

"They recognized him, Mr. C. Do you want them to stop him or something . . .?"

"No but if they're bored, they can have a little fun with

that joker. After all he's speeding and that endangers decent folks like us."

The Mustang was a quarter mile ahead, rapidly fading into the night.

The Town Car's driver floored the accelerator. The car lunged forward like a powerful night prowler. The distance between the cars shrank. The prey moved quickly into view.

"Lenny, hand me that shotgun," Gino said, breaking the silence. "Let's see if I can scare that fucker." Gino took the gun and laid it across his lap. The fifteen-inch barrel and sawed-off stock hid easily in the shadows. Gino stroked it much like the haunch of a well-groomed attack dog.

The cars were side by side. The Town Car's driver eased off the accelerator.

Doug glanced at the passing car.

The night air was dark but he saw shadowed faces staring back at him. He thought nothing of it. Exchanging brief glances with others on the highway was common. His attention returned to the road and the darkness that lay ahead of him. He felt the fatigue of the drive.

The Town Car matched Doug's speed exactly as both hurled into the chilly night air. A blast of icy wind blew through the car as Gino rolled down the window.

"Gino, you really going to shoot at that guy?" Lenny asked in surprise.

"No, I just want to see him sweat a bit. This ought to be really choice."

"Can you get a bit closer?" Gino asked the driver as he inched the shotgun from the darkness and out of the window like a patient, coiled cobra.

The cars drove side by side.

Doug noticed the other car getting dangerously close to

the white line and his front fender.

He stole a quick glance and reacted instantly. His mind raced. *Oh, my God, that guy's aiming a shotgun out the window! It's a foot from my head.*

His right leg stiffened as he stood on the accelerator.

The sports car leapt forward with a screech and sped away from deadly metal eyes. Instantly, he was a car length ahead of them. He glanced to the left.

Their headlights reflected in his side mirror. He pressed his foot to the floor, watching the needle on the speedometer climb. It was at 95, then 100.

Doug watched in the mirror as they accelerated toward him. His car was ahead but theirs closed on him fast.

At 105 miles per hour, the Town Car closed the gap from thirty feet to twenty. When their speed was at 108 miles per hour, the gap narrowed a bit more.

As the other car moved closer, Doug's worry began. Every second the distance narrowed by only inches as they shot along the highway like two missiles.

Doug spoke to the Mustang as if it might respond to his seductive pleas. "Come on baby! If you've got any more to give, let me have it now."

At 110 miles per hour, additional speed came much too slowly from the Mustang. With the glare of headlights to his left, it became painfully clear that he could not outrun them.

With their front bumpers only four feet apart Gino was ready and turned slightly in his seat. The stock of the shotgun rested on his right thigh.

The car's doors were not quite aligned. The driver shot a quick glance at the Mustang as he inched closer.

At 118 miles per hour the cars drove neck and neck.

A wisp of movement to Doug's left caught his eye. He

turned as Gino raised the shotgun again.

Everything went into slow motion. Fortunately for Doug the shotgun had not yet been aimed.

The barrel pointed slightly upwards and away from him. He glanced quickly to the front and then back to the left. The gun was now only three feet away.

He saw a face hidden among the shadows but could not distinguish any features. Death loomed like a rabid dog.

His action seemed to take an eternity as Doug jerked his steering wheel toward the Town Car.

The impact was immediate and powerful.

He jerked it straight again. Ear-shattering squeals pierced the air as rubber ripped from his tires.

A deafening thud echoed through the night. In a heart-beat the flash of the shotgun and explosion of pellets blasted impotently over the top of the Mustang.

The two cars brushed roughly in the night much like for-bidden lovers stealing a hidden caress.

The three men were startled by the sudden impact. The car swerved wildly as the driver tried frantically to keep it under control. There was stunned silence.

With his foot firmly on the gas pedal, Doug watched the Town Car swerve wildly on the shoulder. He hoped they had lost control.

"God damn it, Gino!" Lenny shouted. "This has gone much too far. You said you only wanted to scare him. What the hell did you call that? I call it stupid!"

"Look, I didn't mean to shoot. It was an accident. I think that guy's trying to start something else with us. Mr. C's gonna be pissed if we just let him get away with that."

As a lone voice of sanity, Lenny did not give up. "Come on, Gino. You started it so let it go!"

"Yeah and I'll finish it too. I'm gonna get that guy now so shut your fucking trap, Lenny!"

The Town Car fell behind the Mustang by forty feet but the driver managed to keep it safely on the road. Once recovered the accelerator was again back to the floor.

"Hit him from the back!" Gino ordered. "Maybe he'll lose it like we almost did."

Doug's car pulled away but the other driver was good. In barely a second they were only twenty feet back. Doug watched their car change lanes, moving directly behind his.

His speed topped out at 120 miles per hour. Doug could see their headlights, getting closer as they approached from the rear. It looked like they intended to ram him.

Doug reacted, changing lanes quickly. They followed, staying as close as they could. The heavier car slammed into the Mustang. The jarring impact sent it forward with a jolt.

Doug's mind hunted for alternatives. What should he do? He would be airborne for an instant and out of control. He reminded himself, do not move the steering wheel even a fraction of an inch until the tires touch the road again.

He waited for the bounce then after what seemed like a very long second, he felt the road again.

Doug maintained control and easily moved back onto the pavement. The other car was now back about forty feet but approaching fast.

Doug braced for another impact.

His speed was 110 and rising slowly. 113. 116. Finally, the bump happened just as he had anticipated but it was not as solid as the first one. He recovered quite easily and there was another one within seconds.

It was a bit harder but still easy for him to handle.

Gino's anger escalated. He was no longer satisfied with

just ramming Doug's car. Now he wanted more!

As he gripped the shotgun, he shouted. "Pull up next to that fucker. I've had enough of this shit. I'm gonna shoot the son-of-a-bitch."

The Town Car changed lanes and started closing in.

Doug watched the other car move closer. Its acceleration was slow but steady. Doug thought about what might happen next but there was little time before the car pulled along side of his.

He braced for a side impact.

This time Gino had the shotgun ready. He squirmed in his seat. He wanted another chance and sought to make it better than the last one. He hoped to end this crazy game and to do it immediately.

As Gino prepared to fire, Doug saw the shotgun's movement. Without hesitating he jerked the steering wheel to the left, lifted his foot off the accelerator and stomped hard on the brakes.

Tires squealed in pain to stop the Mustang.

Doug's front bumper gouged deep into the Town Car's rear door and fender. He hoped they would spin out of control. Doug braced himself for the unexpected not knowing what would happen next.

His car spun in a complete circle before it straightened out again on the highway. With locked brakes a hundred feet of squealing tires filled his ears and dark billowing smoke filled the air. The Mustang rolled to a smooth stop.

With the engine still running Doug prayed for that to be the end of it! But, it was not over for the Town Car.

Squealing tires, blinding smoke and explosive sounds erupted as it rolled and tumbled down the highway. The final rollover seemed to take forever but it stopped sixty feet ahead of Doug's car, resting on the passenger's door and across a drainage ditch.

Two passengers were tossed out like broken straw men and lay sprawled on the pavement. Neither moved. The last man remained inside the car. There was no fire.

Silence filled the darkness.

Doug's car straddled two lanes of the highway, facing the ditch. To his left the other car rested on its side.

Cautiously, he drove toward it, avoiding the two bodies on the pavement. He stopped twenty feet past the wreckage and got out of his car.

The night air was cold but he did not feel its nip.

Breathing heavily, he noticed his heart pounding like a freight train on a steep grade. His hands tingled with anticipation for what might happen next.

Squatting behind the rear fender of his car, he surveyed the gruesome scene. There had been no movement from the two bodies sprawled on the highway.

He focused on the man inside the overturned vehicle. The weeds along the shoulder were knee-high. From where he stood, he could see through the broken windshield but no one was visible.

With only enough moonlight to see vague, ghost-like shapes, Doug moved closer.

After a few steps he saw the car's dashboard and front seat. Getting closer, he could see something else in the shadows then standing in front of the broken windshield, he could see a man's shoe.

He looked up and down the highway for approaching traffic. None came from either direction. Again he glanced at the bodies; neither showed signs of movement. He thought if they have not moved yet, there was probably little reason to be concerned.

Doug's eyes adjusted to the darkness.

Again he looked through the broken windshield. He could see the man's legs. Focusing harder, he saw the man's body stretched out along the car's shattered side window. The man's feet and legs were extended into the front seat area with his torso and head stretched into the back.

Such rollovers toss passengers around quite a bit. Doug wondered what their final seconds of life would have been like. Watching intently, he saw no signs of movement from this man either.

He walked around the car and looked for signs of leaking gasoline. He smelled it at the rear and hoped there was not enough to be a problem.

Doug kicked at the heavily damaged windshield. After several well-placed impacts, it collapsed. He tossed the large chunks of glass out of the way so he could reach the body.

There was no blood or other signs that the man was injured. Since his legs were not twisted or distorted, Doug assumed they were not broken.

He grabbed one of the man's feet and pulled. The shoe came off in his hand. Tossing it away, he reached further into the car and grabbed both of the man's legs.

He steadied his footing. With a firm grip he pulled hard on the lifeless body. It moved several feet. He could see the man's waist. A nine-millimeter pistol was in a holster on his belt. Doug scanned him for movement.

When there was none, he grabbed the gun and tossed it into the grass behind him. He could not see the man's hands yet so he pulled again.

The body failed to move. It was stuck. Pausing, Doug turned it slightly, then it moved easier. Doug reached for the man's neck and felt for a pulse.

There was none. This man was dead.

Doug dragged the body through the broken glass and shattered windshield, then using his shoulder he carried it well away from the car where it lay motionless.

Moving back toward the car, Doug tripped on something hard like a rock and obscured by the grass. He stumbled. Regaining his balance, he searched for the offending object.

The grass was moist with evening dew. Doug brushed something shaped like a rifle. He picked it up and moved out of the shadow to check it out.

It was the shotgun! The cause of all this pain and death.

Doug held it firmly and wondered what that man had on his mind when he stuck it out the window and aimed it at him. A question he would never have answered.

He decided to check the other bodies just to be sure. He walked toward the first one.

The shotgun hung in his left hand.

In the distance Doug saw headlights come into view. Too much time had passed since another car had driven by. He needed assistance and hoped they would phone the Highway Patrol from the next town.

Doug knelt at the first body. The man lay on his stomach with his head turned toward Doug. A stream of blood flowed from his head. In the fading moonlight it looked black, more like oil than blood, and flowed away from the body toward the side of the road.

Touching the man's neck, Doug determined he had no pulse and was quite dead.

Doug stood. The approaching car had moved closer. He could now distinguish both headlights clearly but it was still a good distance away.

Noticing his strangle grip on the shotgun, Doug wondered why he still held it. There was no need for it now.

He flung it toward the weeds at the side of the highway. It twirled and whistled softly as it sailed through the air, landing with a soft thud.

Doug walked to the last body. He stooped to check for a pulse and recognized the man as one of those who broke into his room the prior night.

He was confused.

A flood of thoughts shot into his head. *What the fuck just happened here?* He was unsure of exactly how but he felt that Mr. C was somehow connected to this accident.

As he stood, he wiped a drop of the man's blood from his finger onto the sleeve of his shirt.

The approaching car was now a quarter of a mile away.

Walking in the middle of the road toward the oncoming lights, he waved his arms wildly in the air.

He shivered. The cold night air finally chilled him.

The dark colored car slowed and approached cautiously. Doug did not blame them for being careful. This was a desolate part of the country and he would probably be just as wary of stopping. The car finally stopped ahead of him.

Doug paused and waited but nothing happened.

Finally the driver's door opened and a hulk of a figure rose from it. The man remained at the door in a stooped position as if talking to someone inside the car.

Doug walked toward the car.

When he was close enough to speak, he said. "Nice of you to stop. This is a really bad one!"

The man did not look up or respond.

Doug stopped in front of the car.

He tried to stay well lit by the headlights. The last thing he wanted was to frighten these passengers any more than the gory scene might already have done.

Mr. C recognized Doug even before the limo stopped. The limo driver had alerted him to the accident a quarter of a mile earlier. Mr. C knew to expect weird things from the men in the Town Car but this scene was a total surprise.

Mario popped the side-door's decorative panel and retrieved Mr. C's hidden shotgun. Passing it to him, he said. "This should be a real treat for you."

Mr. C gloated. "That's for sure. It's been a while since I killed anyone. After last night this will be sweet one."

Mario carried a Smith and Wesson Model 64 in a shoulder holster. As he spoke, he reached for it.

"How do you want to do this?"

"First you get the drop on him and we'll walk him into the brush away from the highway. I'll kill him there so you won't have to bury him."

Through his half-broken dirty smile Mario responded. "That sounds good to me! Just say the word, Mr. C."

With a quick glance Mr. C searched for oncoming headlights. He wanted this to be a special kill, taking no less than five minutes. Savoring the fear of his victim was an important sensation for his satisfaction.

Both directions were clear.

"Okay, let's do it, Mario!"

Mario reached for the door handle on the driver's side of the car. He pressed the latch and pushed it open as the driver took a step backwards. Mario's left foot slid from the car to the pavement. He held the .38 in his right hand.

The hammer was cocked and ready.

"Hold it!" Mr. C interrupted. Disgust filled his voice.

"There's a god damn car coming."

Mario jerked and closed the door immediately.

In the distance Doug saw another set of headlights come into view. He watched the limo driver pause for a bit longer again talking to someone inside the car, then move away from it as he closed the door.

The driver walked toward him.

They stood in the glare of the headlights.

He spoke calmly. "Someone's calling the Highway Patrol for you as we speak. What happened?"

Doug responded slowly not knowing exactly how much of the bizarre story to repeat.

"Well, I'm not exactly sure. We were both driving too fast. They tried to pass and somehow lost control. We collided and I was able to recover. Unfortunately they didn't. That's about it."

Looking toward the bodies, the driver asked. "Do you know any of them?"

"No. I remember meeting one of them in Las Vegas last night but I didn't really know him."

The driver followed up with another question. "Are any of them still alive?"

"I don't think so. I checked them and they're all dead."

Without saying anything, the driver turned and walked toward the bodies. He stopped briefly to examine each one.

Doug stood away from of the limo, waiting for the second car to approach. After several minutes he heard the wail of sirens in the distance.

The limo driver returned and stopped in front of Doug.

The sirens sounded closer and louder. Doug looked toward the flashing lights in the distance. A second car pulled to a stop behind the limo.

"Sounds like help is on the way." The limo driver said. "We'll be on our way now."

Doug thanked him for stopping and moved to the side of the road so the car could move forward.

As Mr. C's limo drove toward the first body, he pressed the down button of the power window; it began to open.

When the window was down about six inches, it stopped and he spoke. "Mario, you will kill that man for me . . . and I want it done soon!"

The only response from Mario was a nod. The window went back up as the car drove away.

The second car pulled forward and a young woman rolled the window down to inquire about what had happened. Doug told her that he was okay and that someone had already telephoned for help. She wished him well and the car drove slowly through the scene.

Doug felt the sting of a cold breeze. He walked quickly to his car and put on a heavier jacket. He waited as the sound of sirens grew louder.

The flashing multi-colored lights from two Highway Patrol vehicles and an ambulance lit up the area. With the extra light, Doug saw that skid marks covered both lanes. They retold the fateful story quite well.

During the next hour Doug repeated his story at least three times. He left out the part about the mob and how he had recognized one of the dead men. The story was already difficult enough to explain without going into those things.

Eventually a handful of cars passed the well-populated accident scene. Of course each one had to stop and look.

Once all reports had been taken, Doug asked if he could leave. Shortly he was back on the road, heading for home, shaken and driving much slower.

The ghastly scene remained in his thoughts and directed them. What a tragedy. What a waste. What a terrible thing to have happen. What a nightmare!

Chapter Three

Waking up Tuesday morning, Doug was only half rested. For the first time since being in Vietnam he felt emotionally battered. He lay motionless for a while. He had been so tired and distressed last night that sleep came quickly. He slept soundly, almost dead to the world.

He was still really sore from the beating two nights ago. The bruise on his left cheek and the one on his chest were still noticeable. The past weekend had certainly been memorable. The first few days had been restful and relaxing. Too bad he had decided to stay for an extra day but he had no reason to be upset about it now. He gave up predicting the future and worrying about the past a few years ago. He could do nothing about either so why bother.

What was that guy's name? What had Ralph called him? He remembered Dante . . . something. All he could recall for sure was Mr. C. His mind strained. *What was the rest? It was quite a long name. Dante . . .*

Well, it was no big deal now since he could not do anything else. After all he would never see those guys again. For Doug it was simple; he would just stay in a different hotel the next time he went to Las Vegas.

Jumping from the bed with an unmistakable pressure on his bladder, he ran butt naked for the bathroom.

During the next half-hour he showered and shaved. Getting ready for work in the morning had turned into such a ritual, he could probably do it in his sleep.

What a comical image! Sleepwalking at 1:30 in the morning. Getting ready for work, then sleep sitting until 8:20, when I would leave for the office. That's not very inviting or comfortable.

Doug glanced at the clock; it was late. He had to get to work. He knew he would be asked to explain his bruises. Then he would endure endless jokes about *running into door knobs* for the rest of the day. Finally he would be flooded with dumb fight questions but he could handle it all.

He started a to-do list for the day. First, he needed to call Mary and get her working on his insurance to fix the Mustang and then to get him a rental. He hoped the repairs could be done by the end of the week. Lastly, he would wait and call Catherine later in the day.

He backed out of the garage and headed for the office.

Dante Frederico de Casale sat behind a long, polished mahogany table. His conference room looked much like the boardroom in a prosperous Wall Street corporation.

The vice presidents and senior executives were all gathered, waiting to discuss the latest marketing strategies or income projections. The CEO stood to get their attention and begin the meeting. It all looked and sounded very respectable but that was not the kind of business Mr. C ran.

His voice boomed. "All of you have probably heard the gossip. So, I'll straighten out the facts about our problem. Some guy got out of line at the casino. Mario tried to settle it Sunday night but the man was not satisfied. On the way home yesterday, he started messing around with Gino and Lenny. He killed them both on the highway along with Guido that new driver."

Mr. C paused, reflecting on the deaths. Pleased with the atmosphere he had created, he continued with the same tone.

"Lenny was a nice kid. I liked him."

There was stone-cold silence in the room.

"Lenny was like my own boy, level-headed, a very hard worker. I knew I could always depend on him. Gino was a bit of a hothead but still a good boy. I cared about them both, just like my own family. They've both worked for me for quite a long time.

"I just can't let this kind of affront go unpunished when three good men are killed so horribly. It was senseless! I will get my payback. Together we will get this guy and I mean get him good."

He paused again.

All eyes were still focused on him and no one dared speak. He continued but with a softer voice.

"Mario, I want you to get on the phone and get that guy's name from the casino manager. Do whatever it takes but get me a name and address."

Mario's response was snappy. "Will do, Mr. C. I'll get on that right away."

"Also, get two of our best for a hit. I want this scumbag dead and his whole family too. You got that? I want absolutely everybody around him dead. I want it done as soon as you find him, then have somebody cleanup the mess. I want nothing left but dead bodies, right?"

"Yes, sir. I'll get right on that and get it done for good this time, Mr. C." Mario was a good yes-man and he enjoyed that part of the job.

"Let me know when it's done."

For years Dante ran only the illegal gambling operations in Los Angeles. Although he was not really the big boss, he thought he was and of course, acted like it on his own turf. There were actually two other thugs between him and the real boss, Bruno Sebastino.

In earlier days, Dante was a violent scrapper. Moving along the eastern waterfront, he made quite a name for himself. Not only was he a dependable enforcer but he was also a particularly vicious one. He would cut and slash his victims until they nearly died, then refuse to kill them, even when they begged. Fear of doing business with Dante was no joking matter.

The years took their toll on him. He looked much older than sixty-three. He moved through the day without exertion but tired much too easily. He was balding and a hundred extra pounds hurt him more than they helped.

He spoke often about having lived a fortunate life. After all he had power, money and respect and bragged that he had never worked an honest day in his life. His friends said he mistook the natural slowing down of his body as getting ready to die and he claimed he could go at any time.

Dante never married nor stayed in touch with any of the kids he fathered over the years. He had lived in Los Angeles for more than twenty-five years. In the beginning he worked directly for Bruno's father but that did not last long since Dante brought too much heat down on the family.

In those early years every job he did got very messy and pointed unmistakably to the mob and that was the last thing they wanted. He was quietly moved into gambling.

The only enforcement he was allowed to do without permission involved minor stuff on the streets and then only when it pertained directly to his gambling operations.

The major reason the mob had not already dumped him was because he had run gambling for the past fifteen years and had made it much more profitable and well-concealed from the cops.

Over the years his clubs had built a strong, affluent clientele and Bruno praised him for that. Usually Mr. C created no problems and that made Bruno happy so Bruno left him alone. As long as Mr. C did not rock the boat too much and stayed out of Bruno's way, things were fine.

Doug jumped when the alarm sounded.

He covered his head with a pillow, not wanting to believe it was already morning. He should have left Catherine's house earlier last night. After dinner they talked and played around until midnight. He wanted to stay and she agreed but he decided to go home so that he could get more rest.

Waking up would certainly have been more enjoyable if he had stayed with her.

He had just stepped out of the shower when he heard an unusual sound. Doug walked into the bedroom, hoping to hear it again. It seemed to have come from downstairs so he walked onto the landing.

He waited for a moment then heard the doorbell ring.

"Hold on, I'll be right there!" He yelled from the top of the stairs. He rushed to find a robe and slippers, then ran down the stairs, taking several at a time. He landed on a loose one and it wailed loudly. He had intended to fix that one for over a year now and made a mental note that he would do it next Saturday.

Doug peeked through the side window at the bottom of the stairs. Two men dressed in dark suits stood at the door. One wore a hat. They looked clean cut enough but after what had just happened to him, he decided not to open the door too quickly.

Raising his voice, he shouted. "What do you guys want?"

"We're LA Police Detectives." One of them responded in a muffled voice. "We have a few questions, Mr. Carlson. Can you open the door, please?"

Doug opened the door a little but kept his foot firmly planted against it. He peeked through the crack as one of the men held a badge near the edge of the door.

It looked like a real badge so he opened the door. The second man also held his badge out for inspection.

Doug backed up and both men stepped inside. "Excuse me. I just got out of the shower."

The first man spoke. "I'm Detective Harris and this is Detective Long. Are you alone?"

"Well, ah yes . . .." Doug said feeling a little puzzled.

Harris spoke. "Are you Douglas Carlson?"

Long stood a few feet back, glancing around the house.

Still puzzled by the duo, Doug responded. "Well, yes but what's this all about?"

"You were involved in an auto accident a few days ago. I believe it happened on Monday evening. Right?"

Doug nodded.

"Some additional questions have come up since then. Maybe you can help us out? Can we sit for a few minutes?"

Doug inched into the living room, not knowing exactly what to say. They followed. "Ah, well . . .. Ah, sure. You fellows can make yourselves comfortable. Sit anywhere."

Long strolled around the room like he was looking for something. Harris sat in a stuffed chair and Doug sat on the sofa directly across from him.

Harris started the conversation. "There were three fatalities in that other vehicle. Do you remember that?"

"Yes, that bothered me all the way home and most of yesterday too. The sight of it still comes back to me now and then. Dead bodies really make me uncomfortable."

Harris nodded. "Well, Mr. Carlson, after looking over the reports I can't seem to find any statement from you regarding whether or not you knew the men in the other car. There isn't anything stated one way or the other. Did you know those guys?"

"I'm quite sure I mentioned that at the scene but no . . . I didn't know any of them." Doug shook his head, thinking that the added emphasis would sustain his lie.

"Okay, have you at any time in the past ever seen, met or had any type of acquaintance what-so-ever with any of them in any other way?"

"I don't think so. You know, I didn't really get that good a look at them after the accident."

Doug knew he was in trouble when he first made up the excuse of not knowing them. He wished he had not.

"Well, we thought you might have seen their faces better before the accident."

"No, it all happened so fast. Suddenly, their car was out of control. I barely had time to keep control of my own."

"So, you didn't know these guys prior to the accident?"

"I think that's what I just said." Doug replied.

Harris stared at Doug like he expected something else.

"I'm not sure I like this!" Doug said. "Are you trying to insinuate that maybe I caused that accident?"

"Well, yes but that's not really our concern for the moment. Those three guys were well-known local mobsters. They're just small-fries, basically petty hoodlums."

Doug could not hold back anymore. "I don't care if one of them was the local Godfather. I still didn't know them. What's going on here?"

Detective Long moved out of sight behind Doug. Suspicious of what he might be doing, Doug turned to watch him.

Long just stared so Doug turned to face Harris again.

Harris leaned forward. "We're concerned for your safety,

Mr. Carlson. Where exactly did you fit into that picture?"

Doug did not have a chance to answer before Harris went on but in a much firmer voice.

"The highway patrol found a professionally customized shotgun in the weeds at the scene and that nice little beauty has your finger prints all over it."

Silently Doug gasped, trying not to show his surprise.

There was no reason to deny it any longer. He needed to level with them before he had major troubles with the law. Getting the story out in the open would also ease his mind.

He glanced at Long who wrote something in a notepad. Doug knew it was about him and surmised that was the reason why two detectives were always assigned to a crime scene. One talked to the suspect; the other took notes.

Doug knew he had failed to hide his surprise, when Harris inquired. "Mr. Carlson, you okay? It looks as if that shotgun was quite a shock. Can you tell us anything about it?"

"I don't know." Doug said uncomfortably. "Should I get an attorney here with me?"

"Not unless you're involved with them."

Although not completely sure that he should trust these men, he decided to tell them the truth. "I'm not. I only met those guys briefly in Las Vegas."

"So, you had no business of any kind with them?"

"That's absolutely right. I accidentally spilled a drink on a man they called Mr. C. Later that night three of them beat the shit out of me in my room. The next day they probably noticed me on the highway. One of them tried to shoot me with that fancy shotgun."

Long spoke for the first time. "You mean the shotgun that was found at the scene?"

"Yes. At first I tried to outrun them but I couldn't. They

rammed me several times with their car and then tried to run me off the road. Somehow I lucked out, you know, in being able to make them lose control of their car."

Harris inquired. "So, after all of that, why did you even bother to stick around?"

"It seems like a really dumb thing to do now but that's what you're supposed to do, right? I've never had any other trouble with the law."

"Well, Mr. Carlson, I don't think you're in trouble now. You did the right thing by discussing these details. We have a better idea of what actually happened. Why didn't you tell all this to the officers at the scene?"

Doug breathed a sight of relief and started to relax.

"I was afraid to tell anyone because I didn't want to be arrested on the spot. I wasn't sure I could explain it this easily. I'm still not convinced that telling you the whole story was the right thing to do."

"Well, Mr. Carlson, the LAPD has no plans to take any further action on this matter. This visit was strictly informational. However, reports involving organized crime are routinely forwarded to the Feds but I can't see why they would have a problem with your version of the story. They shouldn't contact you unless they have more questions so I wouldn't worry."

Harris stood and handed Doug one of his cards before both men left. Doug looked at his watch. It was getting late. He dressed quickly and drove to the office.

Mario knocked on the door.

It was a few minutes before noon and he knew Mr. C always took his lunch on the third floor patio. The Brentwood estate was large enough that Mario sometimes had difficulty finding Mr. C who liked it there, high in the trees. He felt insulated from everything happening below.

One could hear shouts from ground level but little else.

Mario knocked again only louder.

A clearly irritated Mr. C shouted. "Come on in, Mario, since I can't ignore you any more."

Mario opened the door and spoke. "I'm sorry to bother you, Mr. C but I have the information you wanted from the casino. You know, about that guy."

Mr. C's irritation turned to pleasure. "Okay, just tell me what you got and don't take all day."

"That guy's name is Douglas J. Carlson and I have his home address too. He lives over near the ocean. I think it's a house; that'll make everything a whole lot cleaner."

"Have you got the shooters lined up yet?"

"Yes, sir. I have the same two guys we used in Phoenix last month and they agreed to do this job for the same price." Mario grinned, seeking recognition that he had hired them again for only fifty thousand dollars.

Mr. C ignored him. "Do they understand they're doing everybody in the house?"

"Yes, they agreed to do that too."

"Fine. Who do you have for cleanup?"

Mario hesitated. "I thought we might use Jess. He's got to learn the ropes somewhere."

"Okay but I want you there to check out everything before he leaves. Have him call when he's almost done so you can meet him. I don't want any tracks left behind."

Mr. C knew he had to be careful doing a job like this. It would cost him dearly if Bruno ever got wind of it.

"No problem, Mr. C."

"Can they do it tonight?"

"Yes, sir."

"Fine, then do it!"

A red van moved slowly down the shadowed avenue.

Its lights were off. Three men strained to read the numbers on the dark porches along each side of the street. Since most of the numbers were unlit, they were nearly impossible to read. They knew they were on the correct street but finding the right house would not be easy.

The driver could no longer contain his frustration. "God damn! How are we supposed to find that fucking house? I can't see shit out there!"

The back seat passenger whispered. "Hold it, I see nineteen-thirty-five. There, that light colored house."

He pointed toward it. "So, the target's on the other side of the street. Right?"

A front seat passenger responded. "Okay, that means it's got to be at least four more blocks down the street. We'll start looking again there."

It was after midnight. The late-model van moved silently through the night.

The driver spoke. "We're looking for twenty-three-forty-two. It should be on the right side of the street."

"There's twenty-three-twenty-eight. It must only be another couple of houses."

Pointing to one of the houses, the driver said. "That one there, that must be it."

The van stopped. Six eyes scanned the shadowy scene. The men listened intently. There was not a single sound coming from anywhere.

The whisper of the van's door sliding open was softer than the footsteps of the neighbor's tabby cat. The man in the front passenger's seat slid out and ran silently to the door. He looked at the numbers, repeated them to himself and ran back to the van. He echoed them to the driver. "Twenty-three-forty-two. Check."

They had both done this before.

The driver compared the address to the one in his notes with a penlight. "Address verified. We have a green light!"

Stately, maturing trees shaded many homes and front yards from the sunlight; it also shielded them from the midnight safety of the nearby street lamps. It was a pretty neighborhood in this hue of moonlight.

The two-story house was dark.

The front seat passenger spoke to the man in the back. "Listen up, Jess! We go in first, check the down stairs then move up. Give us two minutes. We should be done by then. That's when you come in."

The driver added. "Remember, we'll turn on the lights of a dirty room. Those are the only ones you touch."

Each man was dressed in dark clothing. The one in the front passenger seat jumped out and ran toward the house. He knelt at the front door, picking the lock. After several seconds, he signaled the driver.

Immediately, the first man disappeared through the open door. When the driver reached the door, he moved inside carrying a large black bag.

The door closed behind him.

Jess took a deep breath. This would be his first job.

He checked his gun. It was comfortably positioned in the waistband of his pants. After pulling on his gloves, he adjusted his clean-up bag and waited.

The next two minutes seemed like an eternity.

Awakened by a noise, Doug fought continued slumber. It must have come from the street, he thought. He listened. He knew he had heard something but could not recognize the vaguely familiar sound.

There it was again, a long, slow squeak like a dull moan. Recognition hit him like a freight train; someone had just stepped on that loose stair.

He gasped. Someone was sneaking up his stairs. *Oh, my God. Someone's in the house.*

Doug jumped, rolled over in bed and grabbed for the telephone, automatically punching 9-1-1.

He waited; each ring seemed to take a lifetime.

The world came alive as opposites. In one ear he heard the soft rustle of feet shuffle the carpet outside his bedroom. In the other the blasting of the telephone as it rang at the other end of the line.

After two rings, he could wait no longer. He laid the receiver on a bedside table. He had to get out of bed and out of sight. He had to hide! Frightened, he slid out of bed but was unsure about what to do next.

Through the darkness, Doug heard whispers.

His heart jumped again. *Oh shit, there's more than one of them.* He knelt by the bed, pushing one of his shoes aside.

After a second he decided he could not hide there, not beside the bed. Anybody entering the room who turned on the lights would easily see him.

Doug's mind raced to find a better hiding place. Hearing whispers, he knew they stood just outside the partially open bedroom door. Without moving he hunted frantically for a safer place to hide.

None were available. Luckily, the room was very dark and that would help him a little.

He noticed the open bathroom door. As he started to run toward it, he brushed his other shoe near the edge of the bed. Unconsciously he grabbed it.

Feeling cold bathroom tile under his feet, he heard them enter his bedroom. Hiding in the bathroom like this failed to provide much comfort. He was drenched in cold sweat.

The two men moved silently around the room. Each held a 38-caliber revolver with a silencer.

This type of job was nothing new for them. They had done it a number of other times. Often they bragged about doing more than twenty hits but they had only done twelve. This would be their thirteenth.

Cautiously they moved shoulder to shoulder three feet apart. The driver whispered. "I can't see a fucking thing."

Since Vietnam Doug needed to sleep in total darkness. Some shapes could be seen in the room but distinguishing any contrast between light and dark was almost impossible.

After several more steps, the hitmen still could not determine if anyone was asleep in the bed or if there was one or two people. They simply could not see anything at all.

The driver whispered close to the other man's ear. "Don't wake him. Just shoot him, then get close enough to make sure he's dead."

They split apart with each going down opposite sides of the bed. It was still too dark to see who was in the bed. They worked quite well together, staying aligned with each other as they moved along the bed.

The 911 operator's voice broke the silence as she tried to get a response from the caller.

"God damn!" The surprised driver shouted. "Someone's on the telephone over here. That fucker heard us come in."

The other man moved quickly around the bed. Groping

for the phone in the dark, one of them found it and slammed the receiver down.

Doug knew the wait was over! Firmly grasping the wing tip in his right hand, he prepared his attack. He took a deep breath, then screaming like a banshee in the darkness, he charged at the men.

The collision was solid. All three men fell toward the bed; their bodies intertwined with Doug driving them.

As the shoe's heel impacted solidly on the first assassin, he gasped to retain a fleeting consciousness. Doug knew the man had lost control of his gun when it slammed against the wall across the room.

Doug's elbow jabbed the second assassin in the side of the head. As the weight of Doug's body crashed into him, he punched the man in the face with the back of his fist.

The trio landed on the bed with Doug in the middle. The first assassin was out cold. The second one rolled away, sliding onto the floor at the end of the bed.

Doug followed him, hoping to get his hands on the gun. Landing on the man, the revolver was pushed into Doug's face. Quickly he slapped at the gun's barrel.

He groped for control of the gun with his other hand. Even with Doug's weight pressing on the man, he was able to shift the gun back into Doug's face.

Doug grabbed at the gun's barrel and pushed it aside.

They rolled until Doug felt the barrel press into his belly. Dread gripped him as he imagined a bullet ripping his gut.

Adjusting his grip on the assassin's gun, Doug's fingers closed around it. He felt the cylinder starting to turn as the man pulled the trigger. Doug squeezed hard, preventing it from turning. If he relaxed his grip, the shot would be completed. He tightened his fingers.

The man struggled to regain control of the gun. Prying at Doug's fingers, he grabbed the barrel with his other hand and tilted it slightly toward himself. Doug relaxed his grip and a muffled shot rang out. The man gasped, knowing that he had shot himself.

Doug yanked the gun out of the man's hand and quickly fired a second shot at him through the darkness. There was another gasp and the man went limp.

Raising to his knees, Doug looked around the room for the second gunman. In the darkness he imagined a stooped figure in the corner. He fired at the bulky part of a wispy shadow. The bullet found the other man. He flew backwards and hit the wall with a thud.

Doug fired a second shot just to be sure. The shadowy figure slumped to the floor.

Before Doug could catch his breath he heard footsteps running toward the door. *Motherfucker, what's going on here? There's more than two of them.*

Doug took a deep breath and waited.

The third man ran through the open bedroom door and paused in the faint glow. He crouched in a firing stance with his gun pointed into the darkness.

Doug knew how dark it was and hoped he could not be seen. The man's gun was aimed toward the bed but Doug's gun was pointed at the man's chest.

The man took a cautious step, paused and listened for sounds of movement.

Doug froze and held his breath. One second passed then two seconds. The man Doug had earlier shot in the corner let out a low soft groan.

The third man fired. His gun did not have a silencer so the blast echoed throughout the house. The muzzle flash lit the room. The man in the corner was hit again.

Doug did not wait. Rapidly he pulled the trigger twice but only one shot rang out. His gun was empty.

The third man fell backwards. His gun dropped to the floor and Doug scrambled to find it in the murkiness.

He listened to determine if anyone else was in the house. All seemed quiet. Doug flipped on the bedroom lights.

Three bodies sprawled around the room. Blood covered everything. Doug heard a siren in the distance. He checked each body for a pulse and determined they were dead. As he found them, he tossed the pistols onto the bed.

Feeling safe, Doug grabbed a robe and walked out of the bedroom onto the landing. Turning on the lights he dropped the last gun near the top of the stairs. The siren sounded closer as he moved down the stairs. As Doug stepped on that loose stair, it cried its usual wail.

He paused. *I would be dead now if not for that sound.*

Doug noticed a black athletic bag sitting at the foot of the stairs. He unzipped it to look inside.

It contained guns, ammo and other items of mercenary paraphernalia. *Those guys were ready to inflict some serious shit on me. Someone really wants me dead!*

The sirens were now in front of the house.

Doug heard voices yelling but could not understand what was being said. He knew it was the police.

He zipped the bag and picked it up. Opening the closet door, he tossed it inside and closed the door. He heard running footsteps on the porch, opened the front door and walked outside, facing the drawn weapons of a dozen Los Angeles Police Officers.

Doug led them into the house and told the story of what had happened. He took them upstairs to see the three dead bodies. Someone said that it looked like a professional hit.

During the next several hours, Doug told them everything he could remember except for the black bag and its deadly contents. Once the ambulances had left, one of Doug's neighbors came by to check that he was okay.

At 4:10, he finally noticed the time. The bodies had been removed to the morgue. Only a rookie investigator and two photographers remained at the scene.

Doug found a phone book in the kitchen and looked up the number of the Ocean View Motel. He packed a few personal things for the night, tossed everything, including the black bag, into the trunk of his car and drove away.

Chapter Four

The wake-up call from the motel's operator arrived at 8:30 sharp. Doug struggled to pick up the telephone by the third ring. He could hardly keep his eyes open but forced himself to get out of bed. In spite of last night's activities, he had things to do today.

He called Julie at the office to tell her he would be late. Having already received six calls from the police, she wanted to know if he was in any more trouble.

Before Doug finished half of the story, she was in tears and sorry she had asked. Five of the calls were from Harris. The other was from a federal agent named Otis Townsen.

Since Doug had been straight with Harris, he wondered what else could be on his mind? Doug could not remember seeing him last night so maybe he only wanted to confer with him like he had yesterday but what about Townsen? Why were the Feds now getting involved?

After a relaxing shower Doug got dressed and returned Harris' call.

"Good morning. This is Doug Carlson. I hear that you called me earlier."

"Mr. Carlson, you're a lucky man. I've already been to your house this morning. Where are you?"

"I stayed in a motel last night."

"I wasn't sure if I'd ever hear from you again, since you didn't show up for work."

"It wasn't much of a picnic for me last night but I'll be in the office later this morning"

"Yeah, this report's scary even for me. Did you leave anything out this time?"

Doug tried not to hesitate but did. He could not tell if Harris caught it. "No, it's all there for the moment. I can't think of anything else to add."

"Look, Mr. Carlson. Those guys are trying real hard to hurt you; they're some mean fuckers so don't mess around with them any more. Do you understand? Just get out of town for a while."

"Hey, it's not like I'm sending out invitations to have my house shot-up."

"Listen, I just called to let you know the Feds have contacted us about the case. They think you're trying to bail on the mob and of course this Mr. C wants you on a slab instead of letting you get away with it."

"So you've talked to the feds this morning?"

"Well, not exactly. I do all my talking with them on the FAX machine. Those guys are *by the book* cops and that gives me heartburn. A couple of them act like they're new arrivals from Mars so I keep direct contact to a minimum."

"I've already had a call from an agent named Otis. Do you know him?"

"Shit, watch out for that guy. He'll probably arrest you just because he thinks it cool. He was transferred from New York a few years ago and constantly brags about collaring more than a dozen mobsters before he moved to LA. Personally I think he's full of shit so be careful around him."

"Okay, thanks for the scoop. Got any more motivational stories for me?"

"Yeah." He hung up the receiver in the same unfriendly

way he answered it.

Doug's impressions were mixed. *Harris' opinion of the Feds was terrible.* Interesting but Doug knew the best way to make an informed decision was to find out for himself.

He dialed Townsen's phone number and on the first ring, a pleasant sounding female voice answered. "Federal Bureau of Investigation."

After a brief conversation the phone clicked; Doug was on hold listening to soft music from a local radio station.

Following a short wait there was an answer. "LA Crime Unit, this is Agent Townsen."

"Good morning, Doug Carlson returning your call."

Townsen's voice was quite friendly. "Good morning, Mr. Carlson. Are you alright?"

"I'm okay but I could use more sleep." Just saying those words made him yawn. He fought to control the urge.

"I need you to come down to my office. I've got a few questions for you."

"Well, I don't know about that. I've got a lot of work at the office and I'm already late."

The tone of his voice changed. "Mr. Carlson, I think you're in grave danger and my people can protect you." His words chilled Doug.

"Look, I'm worried about what's happening too but I don't think there's anything you can do about it either."

Townsen's voice was firmer. "Mr. Carlson, I'll make this simple. I won't waste your time arguing. Either you come in and talk with me or I'll have you picked up at your office.

"You can make this easy or you can make it hard. The choice is yours!"

"Okay, I'll come down but I think it's a waste of time."

Mario avoided Mr. C several times during the morning. Around 9:30 Mr. C came looking for him. Now he could not put it off any longer.

"Hey, Mario. Where you been all morning? Tell me what happened last night."

"Oh! I've been waiting until I had the whole story from Jason. He's busy getting the last minute details without being too obvious. He says the station has turned into a real madhouse since last night's events."

Mr. C's eyebrows displayed his growing concern. "Why is he involved in this?"

Except for a blank stare, Mario did not respond. His silence shouted the story of how the hit had failed.

"Okay, which one of those guys fucked-it-up? Was it Jess? I told you about him. You were supposed to keep a close watch on him, remember?"

Mario just stood there with his hands in the air, trying to tell Mr. C to slow down. Finally he spoke. "Mr. C, we can't tell yet if any one of them blew it. It seems that everything just went sour."

"So stop telling me what didn't happen. Just tell me what went wrong with the hit. Did they get that creep?"

Mario hesitated. "Well, ah . . . no, Mr. C. It looks like he took them out instead. That's what Jason's checking now."

With that Mr. C exploded yelling at the top of his lungs.

"God damn son-of-a-bitch! Are you telling me that two pro-shooters couldn't get that job done right?"

Mario backed away. "Well, Jason hasn't seen all the reports or photos yet."

"I don't give a fuck about those God damn reports. What the fuck does Jason say happened so far?"

Mario was shaken. He knew Mr. C might lose it at any

moment. Then no one could predict what he might do to those around him.

Pausing to collect his thoughts before he began telling the story, Mario said. "Well, Carlson's police statement says he was awakened by a noise after three men had snuck into his house. He got out of bed, called 9-1-1 and hid.

"Later, when they were in his bedroom, he surprised two of them. After fighting with one of them he grabbed a gun and eventually killed the rest of them."

Mr. C's mouth displayed his disbelief as he visualized the confrontation. Skepticism filled his voice. "You're telling me there were three professionals and he caught them by surprise. How can that be? He gets in a fight with three men who have guns and he kills all of them?"

Mr. C's anger and intensity built as his face reddened. "This is unbelievable! Did each of your guys just stand in line waiting for Carlson to do the guy ahead of him before jumping in to help?"

"I don't know, Mr. C. That's the part no one knows yet."

"You know, Mario, this is so hard for me to believe. Are you sure those guys didn't just split when things got rough?"

Mario defended them since he knew they were already dead. "No, Mr. C, that's not what happened. They're all laying on slabs down at the morgue."

"I just can't understand how he could kill them all. How could a thing like that happen, Mario?" Mr. C fumed but he seemed to calm down a little.

"I don't know, Mr. C. I only know that no one walked away from it except for Carlson."

"Is this a raft of fucking bad luck or what? Do you think we're under estimating that guy?"

Mario shook his head. "I don't think so, Mr. C."

After pausing to think about it, he reluctantly changed his mind. "Well, . . . maybe."

Mario winced.

The thought of failure was too much for Mr. C as his anger flared again. No longer able to control himself, he continued, this time yelling at the very top of his lungs.

"I'm tired of this fucking shit, Mario. Do you hear me? I'm tired of it. Goddamn, I want everybody here at two o'clock sharp. I'll get that son-of-a-bitch or else die trying."

Doug drove downtown. Townsen's office was located in one of those big new high rise buildings. Upon seeing it he thought, there must be fifty thousand people working in that building. He drove into the parking garage and found the elevators. Townsen's office was on the 24th floor.

The elevator door opened onto a single, small room with three heavy security doors.

They were all locked.

One of the smaller walls was covered with the FBI emblem. It was colorful and impressive but cold. Doug wondered where the people were.

Each door had a call box adjacent to it with a sign briefly describing the business conducted behind it. Doug's irritation grew since Townsen's failed to mention them.

He scanned the message on each sign but none helped him to decide which door to choose. Feeling frustrated he pressed the button on door number one.

The call box blared at him. "Hello, can I help you?"

"Yes, I have an appointment with Agent Townsen. Is this the correct door?"

"One moment, please." There was a loud click.

The box went silent.

Doug waited for five minutes and the third door opened.

Two men, both over six feet in height, entered the room. They were dressed in crisp, dark suits.

The door closed behind them before anyone spoke. "Mr. Carlson, can I see your identification, please?"

Doug reached for his wallet. "Sure, which one of you is Agent Townsen?"

Neither responded.

Doug pulled out his driver's license and handed it to the blond man. Inspecting the picture closely, he turned it over to check out the back. Next, he handed it to the second man, who did exactly the same thing.

"Do you have any other forms of identification?" the first man inquired.

"Well, not like that. I only have one picture ID."

"Do you have any of those new bank credit cards with your picture laminated into it?"

"No but I have several other credit cards with my full name on them."

The second man handed Doug's driver's license back and then moved to stand behind him.

The blond man said. "Mr. Carlson, this is only routine but we'll have to pat you down for weapons. Don't be alarmed. My partner will do it from the back. Stand up straight, please. Hold out your arms and spread your feet about twenty inches. It'll only take a second."

Doug noticed the agent was cautious about getting too close to any private areas, yet lingered to feel several objects inside of his pockets. *This is an over reaction to a face to face meeting. What's Townsen so worried about?*

The first man stepped toward the door. He punched in a security code and the door opened with a sharp beep.

They led Doug through a maze of hallways and up two flights of stairs. He was certain he would never find his way out of the building without assistance.

Eventually, they arrived at the door of an interior office. The three of them walked into the room without knocking.

A redheaded man sat at a large desk that looked more like a worktable. His jacket hung on an adjacent chair. There was a stack of papers in front of him and a water pitcher with several glasses near one end of the table.

He did not look up but instead motioned for Doug to take the seat prepared for him.

Doug sat directly in front of Townsen but back several feet from the table. One man stood directly behind him. The other one stood to his right.

If Townsen was trying to psyche Doug by not looking up, he was doing a damn good job. He felt fear as it rippled across his neck. Any expectation of a friendly meeting was completely gone.

His imagination struggled with the possibilities. What had he walked into here? This was just about as scary as dealing with that mob character.

Finally Townsen looked up from his work and spoke inquiringly. "Mr. Carlson?"

Doug nodded, noticing that Townsen then moved both of his hands off the table and into his lap.

"I'm Agent Townsen. Looks like you've been busy these past few days and very effective too. Let's see . . . my tally shows Carlson 6, Sebastino 0."

"What are you talking about? What's all that mean?"

"Don't bull-shit me, Carlson. Keep this up and we won't be friends for much longer."

Doug threw up his hands in frustration. "Look. I don't

have a clue about any of this so are you going to continue the hard-ass routine or tell me what's going on?"

Townsen did not respond as he waited for Doug to continue. He did not. Both men stared into the another's eyes.

Finally, Townsen gave in. "Okay. I'll level with you. It's clear to us that you're somehow connected with the mob but we're not exactly sure how. In addition we can't figure out why no one's ever heard of you before now.

"Nevertheless, it looks like you're trying to bail on them and they're not buying it. That's why you're having all this trouble. They want you dead."

Doug remembered Harris had said to expect something like this from Townsen so in a raised voice he explained. "Boy, have I got a news flash for you, Townsen. I am not with them and I never have been! I ran into those guys for the first time last Sunday night in Las Vegas."

Townsen shot back.

"So, why's the mob made two attempts on you, wrecking your car and then shooting up your bedroom?"

"That thing on the highway was just coincidental. They saw me and thought they could fuck with me. It simply got out of hand. That's all."

"Okay, wise-ass. What about their hit attempt on you last night? How do you explain that?"

Doug's response was a lie but he hoped Townsen would not figure it out. "As lame as it sounds, I think it was probably just the wrong address. I've heard that kind of shit happens all the time. It's quite easy to do in a neighborhood as dark as mine. I've even heard the police sometimes make those kinds of mistakes. You ever heard that?"

Doug smiled, feeling he had landed a solid punch.

"You don't expect me to buy into that lame horseshit, do

you, Mr. Carlson? Get real."

Doug felt frustration seize his senses. "If you're asking me for explanations, I don't have a better one. Do you?"

"Okay, Pal, I say it happened this way."

Townsen shuffled some papers and continued. "You and your mob buddies were partying in Las Vegas. Something happened and you got pissed. On the other hand, maybe they got pissed at you. What was it about . . . money, a screwed-up job, maybe a dame . . .."

"That's ridiculous."

"So, does that mean you're not denying it?"

"Of course, I deny it! Your imagination has been working overtime on this."

Doug's mouth felt dry. He rubbed his hand over rough lips to conceal his growing anxiety.

Townsen continued. "Next, I believe that on the way home they tried to take you out instead of having you split-up their happy family."

Doug's mind raced for rebuttal answers. "Look if I was with those guys, then wouldn't I have been in the same car with them? You do know that I was in my own car out there in the desert, right?"

"Sure, that's simple to explain. You drove to Vegas and met them there. You had a falling out. You left first. They caught up with you on the highway. It's as plain as the nose on your face."

Doug had had enough. "Well, not to me. This is nonsense. I'm out of here!"

He stood up and immediately something pressed hard into his lower back. It felt like a gun from the agent who stood behind him.

He froze in place.

"Sit down, Mr. Carlson. We're not done, yet."

Doug felt he would not win that kind of showdown. Still standing, he held his hands up at shoulder height. His palms faced Agent Townsen.

"Okay, take it easy. I've changed my mind. We can talk a while longer."

He sat back down in the chair.

Holding the arms of the chair, he turned slowly to look at the man standing behind him. The blond agent held a pistol in his right hand. Leaning back in the chair, his attention returned to Townsen.

Townsen spoke, shaking his head. "Mr. Carlson, don't get stupid like that again."

Doug maintained his composure but did not like it. He responded politely. "No problem."

Townsen continued. "Here's what I think.

"I think you're a mob shooter, you know, a Hitman, who has managed to stay unknown and out of sight. That's why no one has ever heard of you until now and it seems to me that you must be damn good at your job too!

"I think you've started a one-man war with the mob and you're winning. That's exactly what I think."

"Where in hell did you get all this shit? I'm nothing but a goddamn banker. If there's a war going on with the mob, they'll probably bury my ass and do it pretty fucking soon!"

Townsen finally had the opening he wanted.

"Well, I was hoping you'd say something like that. I've been looking for something on Bruno Sebastino for a long time. He's very well-protected 24-hours a day so I need an insider who's willing to help us out."

"No way! You have this all wrong, buster. Let me say it clear enough even for you. I am not with the mob. When dealing with that kind of shit, I'm only a lightweight civilian. What's happening between the mob and me is nothing but a big fucking misunderstanding."

"Well, it's a misunderstanding that'll probably get you killed. Look, . . . we're offering to work with you, to help protect you and to get you out of this mess if we can . . . but, you'll have to help us too."

"I'm telling you I don't have the connections you think I do and I can't be of any real help to you."

"We're willing to take that chance. What can you offer us now, anything?"

"I don't think you're hearing what I'm saying. I'm not with the mob. I never have been. No way, no how! There is very little more I can add."

"But, there is more?"

"Well, . . . not that much but even then, I'd have to think about it first."

"So, there is more but you'll need to think about it for a while. Sort of like sifting through it all, before you decide what you can share with us?"

"Well, not exactly but yes, that's close enough."

"Okay, here's my number." Townsen raised one of his hands from beneath the table. He picked up a card and handed it to Doug. It had a phone number written in ink. He moved his hand back out of sight and into his lap.

Townsen continued. "Call me with anything that helps us nail Sebastino. My personal access code is D-1-2-2-3. Don't forget it. When you need help, the operator will track me down with that code. I expect to hear from you!"

"Let's see if I understand this. You're providing me with assistance to fight the mob and your private access code to call you directly for that help."

He nodded his approval. "That's about it, Sport. You got any more questions?"

"I don't believe this. It's like you haven't heard a word I've said but this'll do just fine. What have I got to lose?"

"Your life!" Townsen answered.

Townsen spoke to the man standing next to Doug. "Take him back to the lobby."

The agent standing behind Doug grabbed his shoulders and almost lifted him from the chair. Doug thought about what Harris had confided to him about Townsen. Now that he had met the man it sounded quite strange.

Walking through the door, Doug glanced back into the room as Townsen took a .45 automatic pistol from his lap, laid it on the table and returned to the work in front of him.

Several hours after learning of the bungled hit Mr. C was still hot about it. That was how he acted whenever he failed to get his way. His blood pressure was too high but that never stopped him. With six men already dead, he had to finish playing out his powerful mobster facade, whether it was real or not!

Everybody was there, even the three new punks from the strip who did numbers for him. Two of them were brothers and both were as dumb as a box of rocks. If any of his people were still on the street, it was only because nobody contacted them or they failed to respond to their beeper. Not answering a page meant big trouble for them later.

Nobody knew for sure exactly who was missing or how they all crowded into the small conference room. The count was twenty-one hoodlums but only eight could be counted-on in a pinch or for the fight that lay ahead for Mr. C.

Every chair was filled. Several attendees stood near the door. A couple of men even sat on the floor and leaned back in the few empty spaces along the wall. This was an odd bunch of fellows.

The chatter was low. Mario stood near double doors and watched for Mr. C's arrival.

Suddenly, Mario sprang into action. He moved toward an overstuffed chair at one end of the room and waved its occupant to a standing position without disagreement. This meant Mr. C was coming down the hall.

Mr. C appeared in the open doors, dressed like he was planning to attend a formal dinner.

Instantly the room hushed. This kind of image and formality was important to Mr. C. He walked into the room and paused to survey the faces.

He moved to the empty chair and halted in front of it. He made eye contact with several. They exchanged brief nods.

He sat and began softly.

"Since Sunday we've been attacked twice. There have been several deaths. At first it looked like one man but so much damage has been done that we believe others are involved and actively helping him. The only thing we know for sure is that they are professionals."

The room was quiet.

Every man responded to this tale of woe but each was affected for different reasons. They all had a personal stake in Mr. C's success. Sure, he engaged in criminal activities but no one questioned his right to make money any way he could. So, obviously, when somebody interfered with his livelihood, all of his men would defend his actions because it also threatened their livelihood.

He paused to build the dramatic affect. When he had it, he continued.

"We're still checking with several out of town sources so

it's not exactly clear yet who's behind these cowardly attacks. I'm telling you men about this for your own protection
since I don't know where they will hit us next. I just want to
make sure that each of you is on your toes.

"I care a lot about each one of you so I want you to be
prepared and ready for any trouble that comes along. I don't
want any more surprises or deaths so stay on guard!"

He looked around the room, panning his head back and
forth. Most of the men nodded their approval.

Mr. C liked that kind of response. He smiled, knowing
that they would back him up no matter what happened. He
enjoyed lauding power over others. For him that was what
life was all about.

He knew that most situations needed to be embellished a
little and this one was no different. Mr. C had mastered those
subtle techniques many years ago.

He ended the meeting with his game plan.

"Mario will coordinate everything from here. I want
maximum support from all of you in resolving this problem
as soon as humanly possible."

When done he looked toward Mario, who was standing
near the door. Mario immediately took over and dismissed
everyone except three of his most trusted friends.

Mr. C remained seated.

Once everyone but the appointed men had gone, Mario
gave the orders. "I want each of you to put together a hit
team. Get some of the tough guys from the street to help but
I want absolutely no trails back to Mr. C.

"There is a quarter mill to pay for the job. Everybody
who's involved gets a share. The closer you are to the kill,
the bigger your team's portion will be."

One of the men interrupted. "Is this connected to that

shoot-out over near the beach?"

"Yes, that was their most recent target."

"Hold it, Mario. The TV news reported that story a little bit differently. They said it was just some guy protecting his home from burglars."

"Since when did you start believing anything the Los Angeles press reported?"

"Listen, Mario. I don't want to push this any further if it gets the police involved. We don't need that kind of heat on us right now."

Mario knew he would have to lie too. "Look! For your information that guy was the target of the hit because he worked for Mr. C just like you."

"What exactly do you know about those shooters? How many were there?"

"We don't know who they were or how many there were." Mario snapped.

Then someone wisecracked. "Or, maybe, there isn't anyone else. Nada . . .."

"Didn't Mr. C tell you that there were others who he was still checking out?"

The man agreed but retained a disbelieving smile on his face. "Yes."

"Well, I'd remember it if I were you. He has more info than any of us do. Are there any other questions?"

No one responded. Mario walked with them to the door and waited while they said goodbye.

Mr. C rose from his chair as Mario turned to face him.

Calmly Mr. C inquired. "What do you think? Can they get the job done?"

"I don't know, Mr. C, they certainly sounded skeptical."

"If it's not completed in the next twenty-four hours, call Bruno's people. Offer them a half million dollars!"

Around four o'clock Doug recalled how lousy his day had been. Thinking about the phone calls and the trip to Townsen's office, he was unable to concentrate on work.

He might as well have gone home earlier in the day. Then it dawned on him. Go home. Yeah and do what?

He had forgotten that his problems would be there too. On one side he had the mob with bloodthirsty goons everywhere. The Feds were on the other side with some weird, possibly neurotic crime fighter running the show.

It seemed that the LA Police no longer had any interest in the case or even any control of it.

Doug knew he had to figure this out before the shit really hit the fan and somebody shot his ass. Pausing, he thought it might already be too late for that.

He tried to stay focused on his work but could not.

What he really needed was some comfort in this storm so he reached for the phone and called Catherine's office.

From the tone of her voice she had not heard the news so he decided not to say anything until later. He only mentioned that he planned to leave work early for a bite to eat and asked her to join him.

She quickly agreed.

Doug closed his eyes and imagined the photo of her sitting on his desk. There was dark hair artfully loose and hanging around her shoulders. She had a light complexion with smoother skin than most thirty-eight year old women. She was nearly a half a foot shorter than him but never willing to admit it. College educated with a serious manner about life and a childlike attitude about fun. As a professional woman she had flourished and there were major career achievements. She was modest but proud of herself and her closeness to her sister.

Doug grinned at remembering her big smile and how it had originally attracted him. Her life was happy and her face broadcast it. She had a soft but firm way of speaking.

They met at her favorite restaurant, The Pasta Palace, on a back street in Hollywood. The early dinner was just what he needed since he had forgotten to eat lunch.

By six o'clock they had both finished eating and were ready to leave for her house. Doug still had not mentioned anything about last night because he wanted to wait and discuss it when they were alone.

It was a 45-minute drive but it would be much quicker when all that damn freeway construction was completed. At the rate the job was going it would take another ten years.

They arrived and easily settled down to relax and chat about their day's activities. With refreshments on the table, Doug asked to watch television for a while.

She agreed easily; that was her way.

Catherine did many things to please Doug but they also had things in common. They had similar outlooks on life. They liked many of the same movies and quite a few of the same restaurants. After a while she started wearing colors she knew he liked. With her guidance he did the same.

She was accommodating but hardly could be described as a pushover. She was an admirable woman. That was the primary reason he had stayed with her for the past three years. The romance was fulfilling for him and he believed it was the same for her too.

Doug felt that he could say most things to her and she would still like him in spite of it. She talked much more than he did but somehow that did not matter. He talked when it was necessary and felt comfortable being around her. They had built a solid relationship. It was a committed one but not totally exclusive, at least for him.

Although she had never said it, she acted like she would marry him in a heartbeat. Much of the time he felt like that too but he never mentioned it to her.

Suddenly, the story was on the news.

Hearing the report made it seem like someone else's story. Catherine gasped as she recognized the street and then his house. By the time Doug's name was mentioned, tears rolled down her cheeks.

Silently, her hand reached and found his.

They listened to the rest of the report. As soon as it was done, she grabbed the remote and turned the television off.

She looked at Doug through deeply concerned eyes. "Why didn't you tell me about that? Was it really that bad?"

"After seeing the report, I think it was much worse. Nobody but me really knows the whole story yet."

"Oh, my God." she said while tightening her grip.

"I didn't want to get you involved."

She raised her voice. "Doug if someone's trying to kill you, I think it involves me."

He agreed but still-hunted for a better way to express it. "I know. It's just that everything happened so fast. I haven't had a chance to sort it all out, even for myself."

It sounded good to him but he was not convinced it was the best answer for her.

She seemed to understand. "Well, can you tell me more about it now?"

"That's exactly what I plan to do. I need to talk about it to someone I trust. Maybe then I can figure out what's going on. It's all going so quickly. It's not making sense to me anymore and that makes me crazy."

Smiling, she knew exactly what to ask next. "Well, what started all of this?"

Doug began the story.

"I think everything stems from the incident late last Sunday night. While getting my room key, I accidentally spilled a drink on some guy they called Mr. C. He got upset and wouldn't accept my apology. He even threatened me in the process. It frightened me at the time."

"Did you tell anyone about the threats?"

"No and it got even scarier that night when Mr. C sent his guys hunting for me to get even."

She looked puzzled. "What do you mean?"

"Well, three of his goons somehow got into my room and proceeded to kick the shit out of me. I was unconscious until the next morning."

She reached for the bruise on his face.

"And, that's not the biggest part of my problem. The next day some fellows working at the hotel told me this guy was connected with the mob."

She gasped.

"They warned me to avoid him in the future."

"Sounds like their advice was worth listening to."

"Yeah, I know."

She rubbed his face. "So, you didn't get these bruises in that auto accident."

Shaking his head, Doug continued. "No. By the time I saw you, the whole situation seemed even more out of control so that was the easiest way to explain it. I didn't feel good lying to you but . . .."

She did not let him finish.

"Doug, you don't have to apologize for something like that. I don't think you'd intentionally bend the truth without a pretty darn good reason."

"The auto accident seems to be the next time they tried to fuck with me. I don't really know if they were trying to kill me or just messing around with me, maybe to scare me"

She injected another of her insights.

"I don't see that it matters much now. The consequences of both are much too serious to be taken lightly."

"Well, luckily, I wasn't hurt but it certainly scared me. I hoped it was finished then. After the Highway Patrol finally arrived I wasn't sure about how much of the story to repeat because the last thing I wanted was to be arrested."

"Did you tell them everything?"

"Well, uh . . . no but later I told it all to a couple of LA police detectives. Somehow they figured there was more to it, than what I'd reported earlier."

"So, have the police offered any help or protection?"

"Not really! A detective called this morning to let me know the feds had taken over the case once they had determined that organized-crime was involved."

"Sounds like the police are pretty much out of it."

It pleased Doug that she was capable of asking insightful questions about his dilemma.

She continued. "Has there been any more contact with this Mr. C character?"

"No. I haven't seen him except for that time in the casino but I recognized some of his people both times. It's sure beginning to look like he's the one behind all of this." Doug shook his head, feeling frustrated.

She quizzed him. "Okay as of this moment, what do we know for sure? What are the facts you know?"

Doug thought for a moment.

"Let's see . . . there's been four situations so far. Everything else we're talking about is just guesswork."

"Let me see if I've got it. There's the original incident, then the fight in your room, the accident on the freeway and the break-in last night. Right?"

She smiled but the sparkle in her eyes was missing.

"Yeah, . . . but where's this going?"

"It seems to me there must be some logical connections in all this mess. That's what we've got to figure out."

She understood exactly what Doug had been trying to do.

Happily, he told her so. "That's good! I'll go along with that. What's next?"

A smile of satisfaction returned to her face.

"Do you really believe that Mr. C's with the mob? If so, that's a very critical piece of the puzzle."

Not wanting it to be true, he hesitated. "I'm not entirely convinced but seems like he is . . .."

Suddenly, Doug remembered the bag. Excitement filled him. "Wait a minute! I forgot to mention something. I have a bag they brought to my house last night. It's full of guns, ammo and other stuff like that. Now that I think about it, finding that bag convinces me."

Doug paused, waiting to emphasize his new conclusion. "Okay, I'm sure. He's with the mob."

She squeezed his hand as she spoke. "Doug that bothers me even more. Tell me what happened last night."

He thought for a couple seconds then began. "Well, let's see. It was after midnight. I heard one of them step on that loose stair. That woke me up and probably saved my life. I called the police but there was no time to talk. There were three of them and each had a gun. Luckily, only two came into the bedroom in the beginning."

She stared, eyes welling up, entranced by the details.

"I hid in the bathroom. When they realized I was not asleep in the bed, I attacked two of them. We fought and as I struggled with one of them for control of his gun it went off and he was shot.

"I grabbed the gun and quickly shot the other two. Blood was everywhere, even on the walls."

Catherine made a face of disgust. Doug reached for his bottle of beer and took a sip, then a second longer one.

During the pause she sipped on hers too.

"Later, I found the bag of guns at the bottom of the stairs. After looking inside, I tossed it into the closet. The police were already at the door so I let them in."

She followed up. "Doug, that was such an ordeal! Why didn't you call me?"

"It was late, I just wanted to go to sleep. I thought about calling but finally decided not to. I wish now that I had."

"Me too."

They each took another sip of beer.

She relaxed her grip on his hand and leaned back on the sofa. She smiled as he got up and went to the bathroom.

When he returned she said. "So, where's that bag now?"

"It's in the trunk of the rental car. Why . . .?"

"Those guns will come in handy if you're forced to defend yourself again."

"You're right but I was hoping to avoid that."

Even as Doug spoke he knew the mind-sets of war and that of a peaceful everyday life were quite different. Having already experienced war, he did not want to experience it again over something as petty as a spilled drink.

"Do you think that's realistic?"

"Well, maybe not but I don't think my luck's going to hold out forever. This guy has probably got a lot more hired guns to send after me. Eventually, ..."

Excitedly, she interrupted. "You know that might just be the key, his willingness to send more people after you."

Doug was surprised because her comment seemed to come from left field. "What . . .?"

Catherine explained.

"Well, there's got to be some point where it becomes too costly for him to keep trying to kill you. My God, six people have already died! Hopefully, he won't be able to sustain those kinds of losses much longer."

As crazy as it sounded, it was a long shot and only half convinced him. "That sounds reasonable but I don't think it works that way, Catherine. Remember that we are talking about the mob here. That's what they do!"

She replied simply. "Okay," then smiled, stood up and went to the kitchen to get another beer.

Doug was puzzled because he could not tell if she was giving up the argument or simply had something else to do.

He leaned back on the sofa and closed his eyes.

She was good at handling crisis. Doug had seen it before but had failed to fully register it. Her growing up in a strong secure family had added much to her character.

A couple of minutes later he felt her auburn hair sweep gently across his face. Without opening his eyes, he knew her face was within inches of his. She had done that before while standing behind him.

He opened his eyes and there she was.

Through her big smile she whispered. "Hey, Sailor, . . . looking for a good time?"

"Well, Lady, didn't anyone ever tell you that Jarheads are not Sailors?"

She continued the fantasy. "Yes but most of the time you've got to make those Jarheads mad, just to get their full and undivided attention."

"So, are you asking for some attention?"

"I am if you are?"

Doug kissed her cheek instead of delivering the next line of their usual script.

Awkwardly, his arms encircled her head and pulled her into an upside-down embrace. As their faces brushed, he whispered. "I'd like that but we need to talk a bit longer."

He detected a faint sigh during her nod.

Her locks brushed his face again as she raised her head and moved to a seat on the sofa next to him.

Trying to reduce the anxiety level, the discussion turned briefly to other things. She told a cute joke she had heard in the office. They talked about several other happenings that day on her job. After several minutes, they were ready to move past the small talk.

Her next question was about his visit with the Feds.

They agreed that Doug should stay away from his house until this problem was resolved.

Although it might be dangerous, he had to go back that evening for a few extra things, mostly clothing.

Catherine wanted them to be together that night, no matter what. Doug described his room at the motel, including its lack of amenities and she decided to join him there.

Around 10:30 she suggested they go to his house before it got any later. She packed a bag and put it in the trunk of her car. Since the motel was closer, they left her car there and continued on to his house with him.

It was a pleasant night for a drive but neither of them talked about its beauty.

Doug pulled into the driveway. Something was wrong.

He noticed the front door was ajar.

Silently, he cursed. God damn, police officers must have forgotten to close the door this morning. It had probably been wide-open all day long.

Then he caught himself thinking that if the mob was after you, this kind of worrying was just plain silly.

Pointing at the front of the house, he spoke. "Look's like someone forgot to close the door last night."

She acknowledged him with a touch of concern. They walked toward it. The night was quiet. The air was cool.

Doug noticed the door had not been left open but instead had been broken. *Why has someone broken into my house?*

Doug stopped to look up and down the street. The neighborhood was quiet and seemed normal. Cautiously, they went inside.

Catherine stayed by the door to watch the street.

Pushing yellow tape on the stairs aside, Doug went to his bedroom. He gathered clothing and other items, filling a suitcase that he carried downstairs.

At the front door, Catherine told him that nothing had happened. Although several cars had passed none stopped or acted suspicious. They put everything in the trunk and drove toward the motel.

A hundred feet down the street another car with four passengers sat in the shadows. As Doug's car pulled away, its headlights blinked alive. A man inside the car bragged.

"What'd I tell you? I knew that guy would come back to his house. Now all we have to do is follow him. In a half hour we'll know where he's going to die."

Chapter Five

Doug and Catherine relaxed, sitting several feet apart on the edge of a king-size bed. Their backs faced the door and a large picture window. Heavy curtains were drawn.

The motel was quiet.

"Where did we leave off?" Catherine asked.

Doug feigned remembering. "Let's see. I think it was something about a Sailor."

She knew he was right but pretended otherwise. "Hey, not that! Let's get back on track."

Since she was serious, Doug changed his tone. "Well, you mentioned something about Mr. C maybe giving up and just leaving me alone. I wish it would happen but it doesn't seem very realistic. What do you think?"

Her response was agreeable and logical. "Well, I can't say that I fully agree with it either. He's definitely got some agenda and that's what we've got to figure out."

"Is it reasonable to think that all this is really happening because I spilled a drink on him?"

It was clear to her so she did not have to think before replying. "No! There's more to it, unless this person is a total fruitcake. Six deaths are one hell of a price to pay for something like that. So what else could be in it for him?"

That was exactly what Doug had tried to figure out all day. Now she had finally presented the question in all of its simplicity. He started the list of possibilities.

"Let's see, they want money . . . and power . . . and status . . . and . . . well, uh . . . can you think of anything else?"

She snapped her response. "Respect. That's a big one, at least in gangster novels and movies."

Doug thought it was a reasonable option to add. "Yeah, that too. But how could I have affected any of those things? It still doesn't make sense. What's he trying to do?"

"Clearly, he's seeing this differently than we are."

"But, how?" Doug was stumped.

To him it was simply a male ego thing. There had already been a tit for tat payback and the score was even. So why had Mr. C disregarded that unwritten code?

Catherine tried to pull it together for him.

"Okay, let's see how this works for you. First, you spilled a drink on him. He gets even by sending his goons after you. That's the end of it, right."

"Yeah, well, at least it is for most men."

She continued expressing her thesis. "Sure and it was that way for him too but something else happened to keep things going."

Finally, it clicked for Doug. "That's it! That's exactly what happened. I should have seen it before. The accident and the shotgun, they're the connections I've been seeking."

Catherine's facial expression joined his excitement.

Doug continued. "Of course. Now it's so simple. Mr. C was somehow involved in that accident and three of his guys were killed. So he has no choice but to come after me again, thus settling a new score."

"So, you affected him big-time with that. The accident just added to it, further inflaming him. That was more than enough to affect his pride, not to mention his professional status. Now, it's probably pushing his get-even buttons really hard. Quite simple, huh?"

She beamed with pride for her part in figuring it out.

Mixing concern with folly, Doug added. "Yep, no doubt about it, I'm a dead man."

"Well, maybe not! Clearly, he's over-reacting so maybe he'll eventually recognize it and change his approach."

"That's nice but in the meantime I'll still be dead."

She proposed a new tactic.

"You need to find him and clear the air. This is only a big misunderstanding. When you find him, you'll easily soothe his injured pride. For a sensitive, communicative man like you, it'll be a piece of cake."

"Catherine, you give me too much credit. That assumes I'm able to find him and that I'll have a chance to speak to him before he shoots me. Don't forget, my last apology fell on deaf ears and it might have even made things worse."

"If that's the case, then maybe there's no hope except to fight the rest of this war with him. I don't want that to happen. He just might kill you."

"Me neither! But I'm beginning to see that as a likely outcome. The only other choice is for me to run from him probably for the rest of my life."

She leaned close almost touching his cheek with her lips.

She whispered. "How do you feel about that, Doug?"

He did not have to think about an answer.

"During my life that thought has been in my mind only a couple of times. I was never able to follow it. Not once."

"Well, this situation is a little different. Mr. C's trying to kill you and it seems that he won't ever give it up."

"That's also what Charlie tried to do in Nam!"

"Come on, that wasn't the same. You know that war is a much different thing."

"Not for me! It's exactly the same thing."

Doug paused for a moment, thinking about his tour of duty in Vietnam. It was hell, an absolute living nightmare. He would never be that same innocent young man again. He would also never trade a single second of it for anything else in the world. Vietnam provided defining moments for him.

Catherine was silent so he continued.

"Killing always involves a choice by either you or your enemy. It looks like Mr. C has made a choice for himself and that decision drags me into his war."

"Those are the scariest words I've ever heard from you. What are you saying, Doug?"

"Well, I'm not exactly sure. There are still confusing issues. I'm not completely sure about that crash. You know, whether they really started out to just scare me or to kill me.

"Maybe it doesn't matter now but I'm convinced that last night's visit was not an accident. It's clear that Mr. C wanted me dead and that pisses me off! Whether it's pride or stupidity, I just don't really give a shit!"

There was increased concern in her voice. "So, what are you going to do?"

"I don't know. Now that Mr. C has made his move, the next one probably won't be long in coming. Whenever it happens, I've got to be ready!"

Catherine just sat looking softly at him as she nodded.

As Doug paused for a breath, all hell broke loose!

The sound was deafening. They both jerked in horrific surprise. The plate-glass window shattered into hundreds of deadly shards. Rapid gunfire exploded throughout the room. From its intensity Doug knew there was at least two shooters, maybe three. The curtains flew high into the air as bullet after bullet ripped savagely through them.

Catherine screamed and fell to the floor as Doug heard bullets impact the walls around them. The room was being torn apart as flying debris buried them. There were muffled sounds as occasional bullets ripped into the mattress.

Everything went into slow motion for Doug as the deadly dance encircled them. He fell to his left side on the floor.

Steadying his nerves, he breathed deeply to get his bearings. Quickly looking around the room, he realized there was no safer place to hide.

He crawled toward Catherine who was already limp on the floor near the end of the bed. A puddle of blood flowed from her midsection. A thin layer of plaster dust covered the blood, removing its luster and adding a ghost-like quality.

She remained motionless as he inched closer. Crawling the last few inches, his body slid across hers to protect it as much as he could.

Doug hugged the floor as the roar of gunfire continued. His arm extended across Catherine's limp shoulder.

There was a brief pause as the gunmen reloaded. A final burst of automatic weapons fire poured into the room. Everything not already splintered gave-up to the fiery assault.

Debris showered them like rampaging hailstones. The entire maelstrom lasted only ten seconds; probably a hundred bullets had been fired and then it stopped.

There was silence.

Doug heard footsteps, running away from their room. A male voice shouted with piercing authority. "What the hell's going on down there!"

Loud footsteps ran across the parking lot to the street. There were muted shouts in the distance then squealing tires filled the air.

Doug heard softer voices coming near. He raised his

head to look at Catherine. Her face was covered with dust and streams of red. The carpet was soaked. Her eyes were closed. He closed his too.

Doug stared at the ceiling without realizing he was in a hospital. Everything seemed normal. He was warm and rested. He smiled easily and enjoyed the feelings of just being lazy then it all flooded back on a thunderous tidal wave.

He realized he was in the hospital and that there had been a shooting. He had an instant flash of dread.

The horror of surviving a mob hit was just like that fucking ambush he had survived back in Nam. Four of his Marine buddies died that day; he felt about as helpless then too! *So what's wrong now? Why am I here? I am not hit. At least I don't think I am. Maybe I am!*

Quickly, he moved his arms and legs, testing them for injuries. Next he moved his toes. Everything seemed okay. He felt his head; it was covered with bandages. He pressed softly for signs of pain. There was none.

Looking around the room, he noticed the other bed was empty. That worried him so he reached for the call button and pressed it several times.

It was a minute before a nurse responded. She spoke as she came through the door. "Good afternoon, Mr. Carlson. How you feeling?"

Doug had so many questions; he had trouble deciding where to start. "Afternoon? What do you mean? I've been here that long. What time is it?"

She rolled her arm slightly to expose the face of her watch. "Let's see. I've got a little after 2:40 p.m."

Feeling a bit embarrassed Doug smiled as he spoke. "I don't usually sleep this late."

She moved closer to the bed. "Well, you were in pretty bad shape when you arrived last night. After patching your wounds you were still unresponsive so we administered a sedative and let you sleep. How do you feel now?"

"I feel fine, I think. What actually happened last night? Do you know anything about it?"

She picked up his chart and read for a moment. "It seems you and a friend were caught in a drive-by shooting. You're a lucky man. You've got scratches and cuts but no serious injuries. You'll probably be going home later in the day."

"What about Catherine, is she okay too?"

"Catherine? Oh, you mean Ms. Walker. She wasn't as lucky as you were. Two bullets struck her, one in her left side, the other in her left shoulder. Both went right through the flesh, leaving clean wounds. I mean they didn't hit any of her bones. She also has lots of small cuts just like you."

The nurse's actions became animated with nurturing assurance. "She'll heal okay too."

"So her wounds aren't very serious either?"

"No but she'll be in bed and resting for about a week."

Doug was relieved. He laid back on his pillows. "I guess we're both lucky to be alive. When can I see Catherine?"

"Any time, Mr. Carlson. Are you hungry?"

He paused to sense his hunger. "Yes, come to think of it. I could eat something. Did I miss the lunch wagon?"

She shook her head that he had not, then asked. "Do you need anything else?"

"Well, . . . how about a newspaper?"

"Okay. I'll have someone get that and a tray of food for you. After you eat you can visit Ms. Walker."

As she left the room, Doug nodded his approval then his emotions flared. *God damn, I knew I shouldn't have gotten*

Catherine involved in all of this. He did not want this horror spilling over into her life too. He was frightened by his next thought. *Now Catherine will want to get more involved.*

The telephone rang and he picked up the receiver, hoping it was Catherine. "Hello."

The male voice was soft and concerned. "Mr. Carlson, is that you?"

"Yes."

"This is Agent Townsen. Remember, we spoke in my office yesterday?"

"I remember."

"Are you okay?"

"Yes. Thanks for . . . ."

Townsen was in a hurry. "And what's happening with Ms. Walker? Is she okay too?"

"She was hit several times and has a lot of small cuts but she'll be fine after they heal."

"Look, I want to keep you alive. I'm assigning several agents to cover you so don't get paranoid if you happen to spot them following you."

"Is that really necessary? I . . . ."

Raising his voice, Townsen shouted. "Aren't you listening, Mister? I want you healthy and able to testify."

"Okay, okay, I won't argue any more."

"Do you have a gun to defend yourself?"

"Yes, at least I think I do." Doug was unsure about the guns in the black bag.

"Well, when you leave the hospital if you don't have a gun within an hour, call me! I mean it, Carlson. One hour or I'll get one to you ASAP."

"Okay!"

"Listen. I really want to nab these guys and you're all I've got for now!"

"Okay, I appreciate the concern. After last night I can use all the help I can get."

"Remember, keep me posted!"

He hung up the receiver and Doug did the same.

Doug evaluated what had just happened. Maybe this guy was not too bad after all. He was certainly driven to capture those mob characters. Townsen had shown them a good amount of friendly concern although he still thought Doug was a mob hitman. Doug wondered if that was a contradiction he needed to worry about.

A young woman pushed a food cart into the room. Doug hoped it was his lunch. It was. While he was eating, a blond high school volunteer brought a newspaper and placed it at the foot of his bed. He ate everything on the tray. The food was actually quite good for hospital food.

He reached for the paper and held the front page in the air. There it was. Not the most important news of the day but near the bottom of the front page. *Drive-by Shooting: Two tourists injured in West LA.* The Times took about a dozen inches to retell the meager details of the story.

Doug laughed at their presentation. It had an unusual slant. How could anybody call that a drive-by shooting?

And what was this hype about tourists? It was like reading about someone else. He read it again not believing it was actually about him and Catherine. He was pleased that their names had not been mentioned.

He scanned the rest of the main section for other news and laid it on the table. He wondered, why so much of the daily press was concerned with people and places he had never heard of and did not really care about?

An older, mostly gray-haired doctor came into his room

to examine him. He looked Doug over, feeling and pressing just about everywhere he could without embarrassing them both. He felt around the edge of the head bandages.

He was not very talkative except for the basics. Since there had been lots of broken glass at the scene, that was what caused most of Doug's injuries. He grinned with pride that they were all minor.

The doctor offered Doug a prescription for painkillers but he declined saying he had no need for them. Next he asked if Doug wanted to stay overnight in the hospital since Catherine needed to recover a bit longer.

Is the doctor implying that he believes Catherine is my wife? Doug did not know for sure but his heart raced at his own thought. *My wife!* No one had ever hinted those words to him. They were not a bad feeling but not true either.

He told the doctor he would be more comfortable in a motel. After several minutes the doctor left saying it would take about an hour to prepare his discharge papers.

Finally he was able to see Catherine but first he had to get out of his immodest gown. He called for a nurse to help find his clothing. Vera was a nice woman who looked like one of his elderly aunts. She stayed for a while helping him to clean his clothes then departed with a smile.

He dressed quickly and went to Catherine's room on the third floor. He walked in and stood several feet from her bed. Her head was turned toward the window and away from him. The other two beds were empty.

He spoke in a deep, seductive voice. "Hey, stranger, you looking for a good time?"

Surprised, she turned her head as if pain filled her body. She responded through a wide smile but altered their script. "Could be but I don't seem to be fully operational."

She looked as if someone had used a penknife on her

face. Many small cuts covered her right cheek and there were several larger ones.

Feeling rage flood over him, Doug's thoughts erupted. *I'll make those dirty rotten motherfuckers pay for every moment of this shit. I swear I will!*

She extended an unbandaged arm. Doug moved to her, getting as close as possible. They embraced for a long time. She hugged tightly using only the uninjured arm. Her other arm was wrapped and bound in a blue sling.

Doug raised his head just enough to see her face. Half embracing her, tears welled in his eyes.

He whispered. "You okay?"

"I seem to be. There's a couple of very sore spots but other than that I'll pull through."

Through her fabulous smile she added. "I hope."

His anxiety poured out. "God, this is exactly what I didn't want to happen . . ."

She could not wait for him to finish before she corrected him. "Stop that, Doug! I won't be treated like a helpless woman, even if I am . . ."

Realizing what she had said, they both laughed. Then she added. " . . . temporarily helpless."

"Well, ..."

Her stern voice interrupted again. "Doug, I mean it! You've known me long enough to realize I won't tolerate anything less than being treated completely equal. It's my life, remember?"

"I know but what I meant to say was that I'm sorry you got hurt so bad. I don't like seeing you this way. I feel guilty for getting you involved. I wish it hadn't happened!"

She calmed and squeezed his hand. "Me too but it did."

"They told me you were actually shot twice."

Moving so that she could point to her injuries, she said. "Yeah, the sorest one is here on my side. I almost cried when you hugged me because it's really painful."

Doug raised himself to a sitting position. "I'm sorry. Is it any better now?"

"Yes but it still hurts a lot. They've been giving me shots to numb only that area. It seems to work for a couple of hours and I think it's about time for another one."

Lightly touching her bandage, he asked. "How's your arm? It looks pretty bad. Can you move it at all?"

"A little. It's not as sore but it's getting stiff. I can still move it but they don't want me doing it too much." She lifted her injured arm about shoulder height just to prove it.

"Okay, you don't have to convince me. Take it easy!"

She raised her uninjured arm to the side of her head, rubbing an injury just above her ear.

"I've also got a couple of good-sized bumps. I must have been hit by chunks of wood flying around the room. One of them actually took a couple of stitches to close."

"That happened to me too but I didn't need stitches."

She paused. "We're really lucky to be alive, aren't we?"

"Yes, it could have been much worse. Those heavy curtains might have helped us. Since they were closed, it was impossible to see us clearly from the outside so they just sprayed bullets around the room. I was afraid that when you stopped screaming last night you were dead."

In a soft voice she said. "Oh, Doug." Then hesitating, she beamed her big beautiful smile toward him. "I'm sorry to disappoint you."

He pushed on her good arm. "You rat!"

Her smile disappeared and in a serious tone she asked. "Doug, was that how it was in Vietnam?"

He shuttered, remembering that there was actually very little difference. "Well, kind of . . .."

She failed to follow-up with another question. He was glad. Instead, she changed the subject.

During the next half-hour they lost track of time, trading stories about how they each felt. They argued playfully over who had the worst cuts or most painful bruises.

Catherine won.

Earlier Catherine's doctor had mentioned that she could leave Friday afternoon if she continued her rapid recovery. Since her wounds were very clean, they would heal quick and be easier to manage at home.

She wanted Doug to stay with her at the hospital for another night because she felt it was safer. She let him leave only after he promised to phone her later in the day when he had settled at her house.

They kissed goodbye and she handed her keys to him.

Doug picked up his belongings and signed the hospital's paperwork. In the lobby he phoned the Ocean View Motel.

The manager was surprised since he thought they had both died in the shooting. He told Doug that after the police had arrived they rummaged through the luggage and debris but had not taken any of their personal effects.

Later as the manager cleaned the room he recovered them and locked everything in a storage room. Their cars had not been moved. Doug thanked him and said he would come by in a half-hour to pick everything up.

Next, he called Detective Harris who was away from his desk. Another officer at the station tracked him down and he eventually came on the phone. "Harris, here!"

"This is Doug Carlson. Do you remember me?"

"Yes. Was that you at the Ocean View last night?"

"Unfortunately. So you've already heard about it."

"Sure, that's the scuttlebutt here today. It also says that the two of you should be dead! What happened?"

"It seems that Mr. C is still after me. Have you heard anything else?"

"No. Since the reports are now all going straight to the Feds I don't know if I can be of much more help to you."

"Well, I don't think I can handle this situation alone. Any suggestions except for leaving town?"

"I've got a friend who was on the force for fifteen years. He was a good cop but didn't like the hours so he quit to do PI work. He might be able to offer some help. Do you want me to call him this afternoon?"

"Sure. I've got to get a much better handle on all this before I end up dead."

He gave Doug the number saying he would also call his friend, Tony. Doug thanked him and said goodbye.

Harris' last words were simply. "Good luck!"

Doug telephoned for a taxi and went straight to the motel. The manager and his wife had already gathered their belongings and the bags were ready to go when he arrived.

The elderly couple were friendly and nice. They even offered to drive Catherine's car to wherever he was staying and Doug accepted.

The manager's wife also followed them in their own car so that later she could drive her husband back to the motel without inconveniencing Doug.

As they neared Catherine's neighborhood, Doug started thinking about their eagerness to help. *Something was not quite right. Why were total strangers being so nice?*

He hoped there was nothing to it but they were strangely uneasy and that was just enough to make him suspicious.

He decided that being cautious was the safest approach so he drove two blocks past Catherine's street before turning the corner where he stopped halfway down the block.

Both cars pulled to the curb behind his. He got out and walked toward the manager who had driven Catherine's car. As Doug neared the driver's door, the manager got out and handed him the keys.

He spoke slowly with a pleasant southern drawl. "Pretty nice homes here. Which is yours?" he asked casually.

For a second Doug failed to find his voice. He looked to the left and saw a white two-story house.

Unconsciously, he motioned with his head. "Oh, that white one there. It was sure nice of you folks to help me out. Are you sure I can't at least give you some money for gas?"

Doug reached into his wallet and pulled out a ten-dollar bill. The manager did not reject it or move away so Doug handed it to him saying. "Thanks very much."

He returned Doug's thanks and walked to the driver's door of his waiting car. His wife slid across the seat to the passenger's side. After he was settled in the driver's seat the car pulled away from the curb.

All three waved and smiled.

They drove down the street as Doug walked to the door of the house. At the last moment Doug turned and looked down the street toward them.

They had stopped near the corner to watch so Doug waved at them again. They drove out of sight.

That was it!

Doug had felt it in his bones and now it was confirmed. They were definitely trying to find out where he lived. *Those guys working for Mr. C were pretty smart. Offering hard working folks like these maybe as little as fifty bucks. They would probably do almost anything for extra cash.*

He ran to Catherine's car. Getting it started in a hurry he sped away, pursuing them. When he got to the corner he no longer saw their car so he headed toward the freeway several blocks away. He wanted to see that they were not hiding somewhere to later watch him enter Catherine's house.

He felt excited as his adrenaline started to flow. It was similar to that of the car chase on Monday evening. He had to find them if only to assuage his growing suspicion.

He accelerated quickly to 50 miles per hour then ahead of him at a traffic signal he saw them. They waited to make a right turn onto the freeway.

Flooded with relief his foot eased off the accelerator.

Doug turned into a parking lot, feeling much better after having seen their car. They did not seem to be interested in hanging around to watch him any longer.

He relaxed, allaying fears they would hide to watch him as he moved the cars to Catherine's house. He was satisfied that they actually believed he lived in that white house.

Still speeding, he drove to Catherine's house.

Using her remote control, he opened the garage door as soon as he turned the corner onto her street. Hurriedly he drove down the block and straight into the garage without stopping. When he was halfway in the garage, he pressed the remote again and closed the door behind him.

His heart pounded with a strange excitement.

Doug had finally made up his mind. There would be no more mistakes! Stuffing the remote control in his shirt pocket, he ran into the house.

He peeked through curtains at an empty street needing to know if anyone had followed him and hoping no one had. Doug was determined to keep Catherine's house safe.

He stared anxiously for a moment to verify that no one had seen him on the shady, tree-lined street. After a couple of minutes he decided the street was clear and that nobody had noticed him. Then he opened the front door and walked calmly out of the house to the sidewalk. He walked briskly but not too fast.

He saw no one else on the street but stayed cautiously on guard. His eyes darted quickly from side to side. Watching closely, Doug scanned the darkened windows for shadows as he passed them.

Doug walked steadily toward where he had parked his car. As he turned the last corner, his pulse calmed and his pace slowed. *Things would be okay.*

An occasional car passed and he tried to check out the drivers. Fortunately, none paid attention to him.

His car was just ahead and still there was no one on the street. No other cars were parked nearby except for his. With his keys already out he quickly unlocked the door.

Getting himself settled in the driver's seat, he relaxed a bit more. Doug started the car and drove to Catherine's house without being overly concerned about the passing traffic.

Once parked in the garage next to her car, everything again felt normal. He walked down the driveway to her mailbox and picked up her mail. He glanced casually around the neighborhood, went back into the garage and closed the door behind him. Before going into the house, he tossed her remote control onto the front seat of his car.

Doug was awakened by the sound of a ringing telephone.

His heart raced. He opened his eyes not fully recognizing where he was. He had forgotten that he was in Catherine's living room. Her telephone had a much different sound.

He sat up on the sofa and reached for it. Barely able to

speak, he muttered. "Uh, . . . hello."

"Doug, is that you?"

He recognized Catherine's voice. "Yeah, I was napping. The phone woke me."

There was concern in her voice. "Doug, it's almost ten o'clock. I was getting worried. Is everything okay?"

He collected his thoughts and reassured her. "Things are fine. I was tired earlier but everything's fine now."

"Was there any more trouble from Mr. C?"

"Nope. None at all." His pace picked up.

"Good, I was worried about that too. Did you get back to the motel yet?"

"I did that right away. I picked up the things from our room and even got both cars moved."

"Boy, you have been busy! Sounds like I probably had no reason to worry so much."

"Well, it's okay this time, considering your situation."

He needled her, knowing that she would respond to any comment challenging her capability as a whole person.

Starting another of their playful scripts, she said in a stern voice. "Listen, Mr. Carlson. You know, I don't have to take that kind of criticism from you."

Since her teasing was meant in fun, Doug played along with it. "That's true but don't forget you're the one who called me this time."

"That's right, . . . but a lady deserves more respect."

"Respect! Are you sure? I heard on the street today that you pick-up strangers just for the fun of it."

This was one of the first scripts they had learned to play. It started when she found out that Marines were sometimes called Jarheads because of their distinctive close haircuts.

"That all depends on the stranger. It's respectable unless he's also a Jarhead."

"Well, . . . what if he's a Jarhead?"

"Then he's got to keep it a secret."

"And just how does he do that?"

She failed to respond.

With silence in his ear, Doug felt her hushed tears. She kept her hand tightly clamped over the receiver so he could not hear her sobs. He waited. After a while he could again hear background sounds.

She had composed herself enough to continue with the next line as if nothing had happened. "He shouldn't take off his shirt and pants until all of the lights are off."

Breaking the script Doug added. "It doesn't sound like you're really into this?"

She sniffled but continued. "Doug, I just want to be with you. I'm so afraid that I'll never see you again . . . that they might . . . well . . .."

She could no longer hold back the wall of fear prompting her tears. She sobbed uncontrollably but this time did not cover the mouthpiece.

"It's okay, Catherine. I'll be safe here tonight and I don't plan to go out."

Her sobs continued. She was unable to speak.

Doug felt she was listening so he continued. "Both cars are safely in the garage. I'm positive that no one on the street saw me drive them there."

The sobs grew softer as she regained control.

"I'll get all those guns ready before I go to bed tonight. If anybody breaks in, I'll be ready and they'll be sorry they started messing around with us. What do you think of that?"

"Doug, be careful! I know you're experienced with guns

but I'm not so humor me a bit on this."

As she spoke, Doug remembered how insistent she had been in the past. He answered simply. "Okay."

Catherine paused. "Doug, when I get out of here, I want you to show me how to shoot so I can hit the center of a target. Then I can help you take care of this."

He was surprised by her request. "You sure that's what you really want to do?"

She was certain. "Absolutely. Until this is over I'm staying close to you so I can be there and help. If this Mr. C manages to kill you, it will be over my dead body too."

Doug did not want her to get any more involved but telling her directly would not work. She would never agree to it. "Catherine, I don't know about that."

She had made this kind of an argument to him many times in the past. It usually concluded with an assertion that she deserved complete personhood, a form of absolute equality in every sense of the word. She was determined to have it for herself and as she described it, for any other woman who was prepared to embrace the burdensome load of responsibility it created.

Although he disagreed with parts of her idea, he knew it was the right thing and the only way she would accept it.

She delivered her crowning statement. "Doug, I've told you before that I will not be excluded from anything I want to do just because I was born in a woman's body!"

"Good morning, Los Angeles! It's six o'clock on what looks like a fine December morning but today I've got something even better for you; it's T-G-I-F!"

"So for all you early risers, let's get those buns in gear. Come on! You can do it! Slide those toasty, warm feet onto that cold floor. Keep going now. Okay, you're half-way there; now sit-up the rest of the way and toss those cozy blankets. Brrr, . . . it sure is cold. Now, run like hell for that hot shower! Oh, . . . that sure feels good!"

"You're waking up this morning with Paul Richie at K-S-U-N, 10-45 on the AM. Good morning, from beautiful downtown LA you are in the shower with Paul every week-day from six to nine. So let's get things moving this morning with a stack of classic oldies. The first of four in a row is from mid-July nineteen-sixty-three. Everybody will remember this super hit by the . . ."

Struggling to find the knob, Doug lowered the blasting volume on Catherine's clock radio. He knew she liked it loud but this probably woke her neighbors too. With the volume set much lower, he pulled the blankets back over his shoulders. Lying there, he napped somewhere between half-awake and half-asleep.

He recalled his chores before going to bed last night. He sorted everything from the black bag onto the dining room table. Seeing them arrayed before him on the table, he thought, what a load of deadly weapons!

There were three revolvers, four semi-automatic pistols, a sawed-off shotgun and a TEC-9. In addition, there were a dozen boxes of assorted ammo with .22, .38, .44 and .45 caliber labels. Most of the extra magazines were already loaded with bullets. Several others were empty.

There were silencers for several of the guns. They looked homemade. *Of course they were! Where do you go to buy a silencer?* There were two hunting knives with well-honed edges. He could only imagine what they were used for!

There were several holsters, two pairs of black leather gloves and three black hoods. There were other items, which he could not identify but one looked like a partial block of

C-4, the plastic explosive he had seen in the movies.

One of the automatic pistols was lying on the table next to the clock radio. It was the one he was most familiar with, a .45; much like what he had carried in the Marines. It had two extra clips and they were both loaded and waiting.

An item on the half-hour news caught his attention. "Turning to local news, there were two more home-invasions over night. This brings to four the number of such attacks we've had this week."

Doug was shocked! He tuned in the newscaster's voice.

"First, at the Ocean View Motel the scene of a similar shooting only yesterday. This time involving the resident managers. Dead this morning is John Morrow, age 66, and his wife Bessie, age 63. Police on the scene stated they died in their sleep because both bodies were undisturbed in their bed. Guests later reported hearing shots about 1:30 but no one called the police until the owner came-in at five o'clock. Upon finding the front door open, he searched for the managers, finding them murdered."

"The second deadly incident occurred in an up-scaled neighborhood in West Los Angeles. Neighbors called police around three o'clock with reports of hearing multiple gunshots. Police responded to a grisly scene where Thomas and Joan Burdock, both thirty-six, along with their fourteen-year-old son, David, had been murdered."

"Another son, twelve year old Kevin, escaped to safety by running to a neighbor's home. According to Kevin, his brother was the first one to be murdered when the intruder attacked him with a knife, attempting to slit his throat. David's shouts as he fought for his life, awakened the rest of the family. Both parents converged on the boy's room but it was too late to save David. However, their appearance created enough diversion for Kevin to escape unharmed. Both parents were then killed by the ensuing five shots from a .38 caliber revolver. Neighbors were unable to identify the assailants and could only describe their car as a dark, newer model sedan. At this point, the police are not connecting the two incidents. In other news . . .."

As Doug's anger skyrocketed, he neglected the broadcaster's voice. He shouted at the top of his lungs not caring if the neighbors heard his anguished cries.

"God damn you, Mr. C. God damn you and your fucking henchmen. God damn, . . . you are nothing . . . nothing but a lousy bunch of dirty, rotten motherfuckers! How can you keep doing this?"

His anger faded into pain. Tears welled in his eyes and streamed freely down his cheeks for the indignities suffered in those two families. Almost inaudibly he spoke.

"Those were innocent people. They didn't deserve to die. They had no idea what was happening!"

Chapter Six

Doug felt refreshed after his shower but details from that news report haunted him. His mind would not stop thinking about those people, the Morrows and the Burdocks. He should have figured that something like that would happen.

He was suspicious and he should have followed it up. He could have notified the police or maybe even the Feds! Somebody would have helped. He did not know what could have been done but somebody should have done something, anything to avoid those massacres.

Now there were five more deaths and a twelve-year-old kid with no parents.

His heart cried that he should have done something. He was the only one who could have guessed what might happen. After that kind of savagery Doug knew that Mr. C would never stop pursuing him. He would continue until he had killed Doug or Doug had killed him.

Doug caught himself with a negative thought. *I must stop thinking like that. No one will kill me, not ever!*

He thought about calling Catherine but decided it was much too early. He would let her sleep a bit longer before phoning the hospital. He had forgotten to eat last night and now was very hungry. Breaking his no-food in the morning rule he fixed breakfast and ate during the next hour.

Doug cleaned up the kitchen before turning his attention to the table full of guns. He picked out a black .38 caliber revolver for Catherine to use at the pistol range. It was small enough to easily fit her hand, yet had stopping power.

He loaded the gun and placed it in a brown paper bag with two boxes of shells. Lastly, he made a final inspection of the .45 automatic he planned to use.

His mind drifted back twenty-five years. He was seventeen years old and away from home for the first time, except for visiting his grandparents during summer vacations.

Doug was immature for his age. He wanted to become a man but had no clue about what it actually meant. Personal responsibility and emotional support were not a regular part of his family's daily routine. He learned all of that during the next few years and he learned it from strangers.

When Doug arrived at Marine Corps Bootcamp, he was shocked beyond belief. He could never have imagined what would happen next. The intense hazing was not a part of even his scariest nightmare. Of course he was not alone.

After the barracks lights went out that first night there were sobs of anguish from other recruits. Although he felt it just as much, he fought tears as many others probably did. By then he had already learned that men never cried.

By the time his platoon arrived at the rifle range, he had adjusted well to the structured life of a Marine recruit. Doug accepted the boundaries and responded well to a whole new set of personal expectations. He learned to shoot very well. That was every Marine's primary duty and a major source of their everlasting pride.

The ring of Catherine's wall phone shattered his recollection and drew him into the present. As he reached for it, Doug noticed the time. It was 7:52.

"Hello."

"Well, stranger. It's been much too long since we talked last. How you doing, Doug?"

"Is that you, Kely?" Doug was surprised and pleased to hear her voice. It had been six weeks since he had last spoken to her. With her voice sounding so much like Catherine's he must have embarrassed himself a dozen times with her but the sisters got a big kick out of it.

"Of course. I'm pleased you still recognize my voice."

"Why? You and Katy have such distinctive and wonderfully sexy voices that would be nearly impossible!" Kely was the only person who ever called Catherine, Katy so he went along with it when they talked.

"Doug, you say the nicest things. That must be why Katy let you have the keys to her house." The sisters acknowledged flattery so easily. Since both of them were pretty and very popular as children, they had had many years to practice and build comfort with their appearances.

"Oh, . . . sounds to me like you've already talked to her this morning."

"Yeah, she called about 7:15. She didn't want to wake you in case you were sleeping-in and that's the time I usually leave for work."

"It would have been okay. I was awake then too. What did she have to say?"

"Well, she's feeling much better and is able to move her arm easier. The injury on her side is still quite painful. She's able to walk around the room without much discomfort and says the doctors told her that she could leave later this afternoon. She wants you to pick her up. Is that okay?"

"I don't think it'll be a problem. I have some plans this morning but I'll be finished by noon. Did she mention anything to you about what happened to us?"

Her tone changed just like Katy's would at his insinuation. "Of course, she did! I even tried to talk her out of it but you know Katy once her mind's made up. Is it really the mob who's after you, Doug?"

He paused, trying to find a comforting answer but none came. "It seems to be just a petty thug, they call Mr. C. With what's been attempted so far, I believe it's the mob."

"Doug, I'm really afraid for Katy!"

"Me, too. I don't know what else to do except to teach her how to shoot since that's what she wants."

"I know. Actually, I'm pretty worried about the both of you. Doug, can you really handle something like this?"

"So far I haven't done too well but I'm meeting with a Private Investigator this morning. If he's interested, I'll hire him to help a bit. Maybe the two of us can figure out how to handle everything better and not get anyone else killed."

"What do you mean by two? It will be three since Katy is planning to stick to you like glue. Doug, she's not letting you out of her sight until everything's finished, no matter what the outcome is."

"That's sort of what I meant to say. You know how single-minded she can be."

"Doug, isn't there any other way to settle this?"

"I don't think so Kely but I wish there was. You can't just drag the mob into court or send the police after them. It just doesn't work that way!"

"What if you and Katy just packed up and left town? At least the two of you would still be alive and we could keep in touch at least every year or so."

Doug noticed fear in her voice as tears formed. She was not like Catherine when she cried. She would continue talking through them. They were only sisters, not twins. They were alike in many ways and there were few visual differences between them that he could easily identify.

He spoke. "I think it's gone too far for something like

that since the mob can get to you no matter where you try to hide. Katy and I talked about it but decided that facing up to Mr. C would be a better solution. Dealing with this shit is just too important for me now. Even if I wanted to, I just can't let it go on any longer!"

"But what if that guy kills you, Doug? They might even kill Katy too." She began sobbing. "I couldn't handle that if it happened to either of you!"

"Kely, I don't want it to happen either but I don't know what else to do. Do you have a better idea?"

"No." She said through her tears.

"Me neither."

"Doug, promise me you'll take care of Katy."

"Certainly. I'll do what ever I can. I want us both to stay alive and healthy."

She seemed to control her tears. After the last sniffle she asked. "Doug, when this is all over, can the three of us go on a cruise together?"

"I'd like that, Kely."

"Good so did Katy when I mentioned it earlier."

"Oh, . . . well why don't you gather all of the details?"

"Okay but you be careful, Doug."

"I'll do my best, Kely. Bye."

After she said goodbye Doug hung-up the telephone but remained seated at the table. *She's a remarkable woman!*

Doug liked her a lot. He often wondered how things would have been if he had not met Catherine first. Would he have fallen for Kely instead? She was three years younger and nearly identical in appearance. Kely's hair was usually shorter but styled much the same. He knew it was too late to think about that since his heart now belonged to Catherine.

Doug found the private investigators number and made

an appointment for 10:30. He called Vic's Auto Body about his car, hoping it would be ready. They told him he could pick it up around two o'clock. Next, he telephoned Catherine and they talked for over an hour.

"Have a seat, Mr. Carlson. Jason Harris called me last night about your situation. I'm not sure I really want to get involved in something like that. Its light-years out of my league and probably yours too. So, what exactly do you have on your mind?"

Tony Miller met Doug at his office door. Doug had seen him pull into the parking garage just ahead of his car so he knew Tony had not been in the building very long. Tony's appearance did not remind Doug of an ex-cop. He expected him to be taller and quite a bit heavier.

Doug paused before answering. "Actually, I'm not real sure. The feds are convinced that the LA mob is out to bury me since they think I'm trying to defect."

"Are you?"

"Of course not! I didn't even know that LA had a mob until a few days ago. I thought that kind of shit happened only in the big eastern cities."

"Well, surprise, Pal, . . . today it's everywhere, weakening in some eastern cities but spreading everywhere. Cities that are too small for the mob have a growing assortment of juvenile gangs that do much the same thing."

"And what exactly do they do?" Doug really had no idea what Tony was talking about.

"They try to get involved in every activity they can get away with. Since most of their activities are not what you would call mainstream, the cops are seldom called. When they can backup their big talk with muscle on the street, they pretty much run the whole show."

"I knew there were organized criminal activities but I thought that was limited to an occasional chop-shop, prostitution, drugs and other illegal things like that."

"When those kinds of operations are located by the police, you can bet the mob's involved. They don't miss much of that kind of stuff."

"So, what do you make of my situation?"

"It's hard to say. Some of the people at the precinct, including Jason, think you probably pissed off this guy . . . what's his name, Mr. C? Or maybe it was just one of his boys and now he's trying to get even."

"Do you think there's a chance of talking to him? Maybe doing that would resolve it and get them off my back."

Tony's grimace convinced Doug that it was not smart to even think about that approach. "Earth to Carlson, . . . that's not very likely. They've already tried to take you out more than once. By now it's serious business to them! Since they have failed more than once, the pressure's on and it's going to get much worse before it gets better."

"Why? They can only kill me once."

"Get real! That's true but eventually they'll start killing people around you and anyone connected to you until they get to you. I wouldn't be surprised if they're not already trying to identify your relatives who live in the area."

"So, it's really that big of a thing to them?"

"Bingo. You're finally catching on!"

"I don't like that very much. They aren't giving me any choice except to leave town in a hurry or to go after them with guns blasting."

"Well, that's half right. They didn't intend to leave you any choice but you spoiled it when they couldn't kill you."

Doug smiled at the thought but his pleasure was short

lived as a knot of anxiety began to grow in his stomach.

"You've added professional embarrassment to the list of insults. Just look at the bad press they're getting. While the papers seldom mention the mob by name, believe me, they're very sensitive to anything even hinting of their involvement. I know this Mr. C's not the mob's main man so you can eventually expect some heat from him too."

"Since Mr. C's the one keeping this going and he's the one that keeps fucking up why isn't the mob trying to control him or at least stop what he's doing."

"Well, it doesn't work that way either. First he's on the inside and you aren't. He's one of them and they know him. He has their trust. They owe him more than they'll ever owe you. Besides all that, he probably tells a story much different than yours, making you out to be some sleaze-character who's totally out of control. I'm sure he's justified it quite well by now and they're solidly behind him. However, he probably won't be able to keep failing much longer. What's it been, five bungled hits?"

"No, there's only been three!"

"Oh so you're not counting the two from last night. They're dead too, you know!"

"Actually, I hadn't thought about those as being hits directed at me."

"Why not? You know you were the actual target, right?"

"Unfortunately, . . . so even running won't help me? They'll just kill someone else."

"That's exactly right, my friend. In the next couple of days you're either going to be dead or I'd say extremely lucky. Even if things dissipate for a few weeks or months, you would still be looking over your shoulder. I don't think they're likely to just suddenly forget about you!"

"It looks like my only real choice is to go out fighting.

Who knows, maybe I'll survive it all!"

"Maybe. Assuming you do, it's still not pleasant, is it?"

"No."

"Do you have a plan yet?"

"No. I was hoping you might help me a bit."

He laughed. "You must be kidding. If I get involved in this even indirectly, I'm dead too!"

There had to be some help he could offer without getting involved. Doug took a stab in the dark. "How about just helping me to locate Mr. C? Help with that and you're out of it, I swear. We'll only talk by telephone after today, absolutely no more face to face meetings!"

Tony thought for a long time before he spoke. "So, . . . you just want me to find an address and that's it?"

"Sure." Doug nodded hoping that he would agree.

"And nothing more?"

"Right." Doug continued to agree with him.

"Okay. It'll cost you two thousand dollars."

Doug knew this job was risky. "That's reasonable . . .."

Tony did not wait for Doug to finish. He knew that Doug's life expectancy was critically short so he added. "I want the money up front!"

Doug left the office with Tony Miller's empty briefcase and went straight to the bank. He planned to meet Tony later when he returned it with the money. Doug withdrew twenty one-hundred-dollar bills and placed them inside an envelope in the briefcase, then he walked to a park across the street from the bank. It was almost noon so people began meeting for lunch, forming little groups here and there.

Doug purchased a soft drink from a street vendor and walked to an empty bench. He sat the briefcase on the ground and pushed it under the bench.

Tony was nowhere in sight.

A few minutes later a red-haired woman in a business suit sat on the other end of the bench. Their eyes met briefly as smiles were exchanged. Doug spoke a greeting as they nodded but then looked back toward the street.

She unwrapped a homemade sandwich and took a small bite. A moment later she spoke almost in a whisper. "Are you Doug Carlson?"

"Yes. How did you know?"

"I have an office down the hall from Tony Miller. He asked me to give you something." She put her sandwich down and reached into her purse.

Doug could not decide whether he should run or not! He reached for the briefcase, trying to determine if this was becoming another bad situation.

She retrieved a white business card and handed it to him.

It was Tony's card and it said simply. "She's okay!" It was signed Tony with a big flair on the end of his name.

Doug looked at her and said. "So, what does he want you to do for him?" Doug was not convinced yet that he should trust her.

"He said he'd left his briefcase in your office earlier today and I should pick it up from you here. Lucky for him I had to be in a nearby courtroom after lunch."

"How did you know I was the right person?"

"He described you, and you have his briefcase sitting there." She pointed. "Since he got his PI license, he really likes this cloak 'n dagger stuff. If I'd let him, he'd keep me busy running all over town but I won't tolerate it more than once or twice a week."

Since she was being so talkative, Doug decided to get more information. "So, he's a very busy guy, is he?"

"Well, yeah . . . I don't see him that much, usually just when he calls me for silly jobs like this."

"Sounds like you're an attorney."

"I am."

"So where's your briefcase?"

"I left it in the car."

"Now, that you know my name . . .."

"I'm sorry. This cloak'n dagger stuff affects my manners too! I'm Dianna Kristos, Attorney at Law." She laid her sandwich aside and handed him her business card.

"Well, Ms. Kristos. Maybe, we'll meet again."

Doug pushed the briefcase toward her. She smiled and took another bite of her sandwich. He got up, tossed his empty bottle into a nearby trash bin and walked away.

After finishing his lunch Doug headed toward Vic's to get his car. It was still a little early so he decided to call Townsen's office. Once Doug found a phone booth Townsen was on the phone in record time, dismissing his usual formalities. "Mr. Carlson, thanks for calling. I was getting worried about you."

"Well, I'm still alive and I don't think they know where I am yet. I plan to stay out of sight as much as possible. Did you read about those two incidents last night?"

"Yes, . . . one at the motel, the other was on a . . . Branch Street. Right?"

"If I had called you about them before hand, could you have protected those people?"

"Probably, . . . yeah, I think so! Well yes, I could have. What are you trying to say, that you had prior knowledge about both those shootings?"

"Yes but somewhat indirectly."

Townsen's tone changed. "Look. I want to know where

you are at all times, Mr. Carlson! Otherwise, I cannot protect you. Where are you now?"

"I'm somewhere on Clausen. I'm going to pickup my car at Vic's Auto Body at two."

"Good, I'll have a team tail you from there. Do you know when your girlfriend is being released from Westside Hospital this afternoon?"

"Not exactly, just later this afternoon."

"Well, it's set for 5:30. I want you there at five. I've had two people on her since early this morning. I figured that eventually you would show up there too."

Doug was pleased that Townsen was trying to cover all of the bases. "Okay."

"Where are you staying?"

"Last night I was at Catherine's house. I . . .."

Townsen interrupted. "That's on Maple, right?"

"Yes. How did you . . .."

Townsen anticipated Doug's question. "I've got a full background on both of you. Staying two blocks from one of those hits is just too close for me. Please do not stay there tonight, Mr. Carlson!"

"Okay."

"Also, get your girlfriend out of town for a few days while we get this situation under control."

"I've already mentioned that to her and she won't go!"

"Well if you care about her, then make her do it. It's for her own protection."

Doug mulled Townsen's words. Boy, he certainly did not know Catherine very well. "I'll try but don't expect it."

"I want you to stay in the Paradise Motel tonight. We can cover that one easily. Do you know where it's located?"

"No."

"It's located at twenty-three-ooh-one Grand Avenue in Malibu. You'll be safe there even if they manage to track you there. Good luck, Mr. Carlson."

"Thanks." Doug hung up.

Each time Doug had talked with Townsen, he was more impressed. Townsen seemed to be fully dedicated to keeping them alive. He had demonstrated more concern than Doug had expected from a federal agency. He already had Catherine protected and Doug liked that. He even had a safe place for unusual guests like them. Doug wondered why Harris had complained so much about him.

For years Doug had been like many people with a sour taste in his mouth about trusting anybody who worked in the government. He knew it was like most other things in life. No matter how bad things were, a few trustworthy people could be found. He was pleased that Townsen consistently showed concern. He seemed to be an honorable man and hopefully he could be trusted even if he believed Doug worked for the mob.

Doug noticed how nice it felt finally driving his own car again. The rental car was comfortable but it did not deliver the pep or responsiveness he expected.

On the way to the hospital Doug bought a single red rose for Catherine from a street vendor. He parked near the side entrance of the hospital and went inside.

"Eagle leader, team reports!"

"Eagle one, lamb inside. Red pony in lane three."

"Eagle two, no bogies in sight."

"Lightning one, ready."

"Lightning two, ready."

"Ground one, all clear."

"Eagle leader, status red. All shooters, lock and load!"

When Doug arrived in Catherine's room, the doctor was still with her. Doug stood just inside the door, holding the rose behind his back. She was dressed in street clothes and sitting on the edge of the bed.

Upon noticing his arrival, she beamed a full smile toward him causing the doctor to also look. Catherine and the Doctor continued speaking but Doug was unable to hear what they were saying.

As the doctor left, Doug approached the bed keeping his hands out of sight. Immediately Catherine noticed. "What'd you bring me?" Her smile flooded the small room.

Doug hesitated.

"Well, I'm not exactly sure what you mean."

"Come on. Don't tease me. I'm in a lot of pain."

Doug displayed the rose. "You faker, what pain!"

Her face lit up. Her good arm reached to pull him close. They embraced. After feeling his warmth she spoke of her concern. "Doug, can we really handle this on our own?"

Assuring her with a gentle stroke of her neck, he spoke. "I think so. The Feds are getting involved to help us."

"Oh, good. That helps a little, doesn't it?"

He asked. "You ready?"

She became playful; "You have to be a lot more specific than that, Mr. Carlson."

"Oh, . . . I didn't mean that. Excuse me, Ms. Walker! Are you ready to leave this sterile, disinfectant-smelling place for sick people?"

She nodded.

After gathering her things he wheeled her toward the exit in the traditional wheelchair ride. A volunteer followed to retrieve the wheelchair. Catherine was eager to get out of the soiled clothing the hospital staff had returned to her.

Doug carried her things in a plastic bag slung over his shoulder. Around Catherine he had forgotten about Mr. C.

She held the rose.

Happily they proceeded down a wide hallway unaware of what awaited them.

"Ground one, lamb sighted approaching exit. Twenty feet and advancing."

"Eagle two, single bogey, forty-five feet west of exit. Stopped."

"Eagle one, dark blue vehicle with three, now eighty feet south. Advancing at five."

"Eagle leader, lightning report."

"Lightning one, awaiting target event."

"Lightning two, ready."

"Eagle leader, Ground one, standby. Move on event."

The automatic door slid open and Doug wheeled Catherine several feet past the entrance. He stopped and helped her to her feet. The Aide took the wheelchair and turned to go back inside. Holding Catherine's hand, Doug took a step and paused to check out the surroundings.

A number of people moved in various areas of the parking lot, either going to or from their cars. One man stood near a light pole. Another walked directly toward them on the sidewalk. Everything looked okay so he continued.

A few steps later it happened!

The man near the light pole threw open his jacket and went immediately into a crouched firing position. He stayed out of direct view by hiding between two parked vehicles. He aimed his .44 magnum directly at Doug's chest.

To their left the tires of the blue Ford screeched as it accelerated toward them. Mr. C's men were determined to get both of them this time. They had planned this hit for most of the day and they knew it would not fail.

"Eagle leader. Go!"

A bullet crashed into the planter next to Doug's foot. His attention was drawn to the man near the light post.

Doug realized that the man had a gun and was shooting at them. He saw a second flash from the gun and heard the plate glass window behind him shatter. Doug had the .45 in his waistband but everything was happening much too fast.

Their hands broke apart as Catherine screamed and fell backwards, landing near a concrete column.

Doug fell to the ground more than five feet away. A second man ran along the sidewalk toward them. He held an automatic pistol in his right hand.

A flash of hopelessness consumed Doug's thoughts.

It seemed they were being attacked from two sides. Before Doug could move, another bullet struck the sidewalk in front of him. Concrete splinters showered him. The impact was far enough to his left that the bullet ricocheted past him with a thud into the building.

As Doug reached for his gun, he heard numerous shots echoing in the distance. He could hear them but could not see the shooters or even where the bullets were hitting.

The running man was now ten feet away. He shouted to Doug. "Stay down, Mr. Carlson. I'll handle that guy!"

There was a loud explosion to Doug's left.

The running man fired twice toward the parking lot as he ran in front of Doug. He headed toward the man who was firing at Doug. Both bullets impacted the car on the right but he fired again and again.

Finally Mr. C's man was hit and flew backwards into the car behind him. The running man continued until he stood over the lifeless body of the man he had just shot.

In the parking lot smoke bellowed from a blue car that had just exploded. Flames leapt from its windows and a plume of smoke rose from it. *What the hell is going on!*

The firing ceased just as Doug had his .45 ready. Keeping his gun out, he went to Catherine's side. Her elbow was bleeding and she was severely shaken, a lot like him.

She threw her arms around him, hugging tightly through her pain. A second later they were interrupted as several armed guards moved cautiously out of the hospital. Their pistols were drawn and pointed toward Doug and Catherine.

They froze in place.

The running man returned and identified himself to the guards as Federal Agent Wilson. They holstered their guns. Doug's hand shook as he returned the .45 to the belt under his jacket. Catherine reached for Doug's hand

With his gun still at the ready, Agent Wilson inquired. "Are you two alright?"

Doug muttered. "Just shook up, I think!"

"Any injuries?"

They looked to Catherine; she shook her head. Doug responded. "Just scrapes and bruises."

Wilson turned and spoke into a transmitter under his collar. "Ground one, secure."

Turning back to Doug, he said. "You two, get out of

here! I'll clean up and explain what happened to these guys. The tail on you will be a white van. Go on, get moving!"

Without thinking they both ran for Doug's car.

Neither looked back. As they passed the limp body of the shooter, Doug paused for a second and recognized him.

His heart raced. *That man's the limo driver who stopped to help me after the accident.* Now he was absolutely convinced that Mr. C and his goons were behind all of this.

He told Catherine as they ran.

They scrambled into the Mustang. Doug started the engine and backed out of the parking space with a screech. The .45 was slid under the bucket seat. Doug could see the hospital exit and the sidewalk in front of it.

Cautiously, people gathered around the entrance.

As he drove away, he spotted Catherine's rose on the ground. It had been crushed near the column.

Chapter Seven

Doug headed for a nearby freeway and then drove south. For the next twenty minutes, neither of them were able to speak. Except for driving Doug did not know what to do or even what to say.

Catherine just sat staring straight ahead. Doug did much the same thing. He looked toward her a few times but she failed to notice him or even to return his glances.

This entire situation is so insane! Thank God somebody was there to help us. His sense of despair drew Doug's attention to a jungle patrol in Vietnam twenty years earlier.

There were six of them on patrol. They had been in the bush for over a week. Doug would never forget the rain, the mud and of course always being cold. On top of everything else, his knee was sore as hell from an accidental fall. He limped painfully for most of the time.

They had seen Charlie a couple of times but had no real contact until that last day when they ran into at least fifty of them. Luckily, they saw Charlie first.

Surrounded by light brush, knee high grass and a few skinny trees the Marine patrol thought it was another small North Vietnamese Army unit so naturally they opened fire.

At first it was an easy firefight. Doug noticed several of them go down. He was proud they were taken out so easily. At least that was how it seemed until Charlie's fire grew much heavier.

Charlie must have moved everybody they had onto the line and did it as fast as they could. In less than a minute the incoming fire was so heavy that most of the Marines were pinned down. Several were able to return fire but the rest just kept their faces buried in the dirt, mud and slop.

The Lieutenant radioed for a huey gunship, shouting that the situation was so fucking hot they needed their asses there twenty minutes ago.

Charlie advanced on both ends of the line trying to flank the patrol. They poured heavy fire from the center, using it to suppress the Marines. No one thought about the Silver Star being earned that afternoon or who would eventually receive it posthumously.

Doug was on the right flank crouched near a tree but it offered little cover. Bullets pounded the dirt around him. Rising he shot a burst of eight rounds but knew it was scattered and mostly ineffective. He needed a much better position. He saw bigger, more protective trees ten feet away.

He took a deep breath and started rolling through the grass toward it. There was an explosion in front of him. He stopped to hug the ground for a moment then rose quickly to a kneeling position. Both knees dug into the soft earth.

Suddenly there were four NVA soldiers charging him with AK-47s ablaze. Doug corrected his position and emptied his M-16 toward them. He watched two of them fall out of sight in the deep grass.

Numerous bullets whizzed past him. Several impacted the tree where he hid. One nicked the top of his helmet. Another impacted the left shoulder of his flackjacket just above his heart. As he fell backwards, he was spun to the left. He lost his grip on the M-16 and it flew from his hands. Another bullet hit the lower part of his flackjacket as he rolled. He felt a third impact in the middle of his back.

Struggling to stay awake, he rolled several feet. Eventually he rested on his back. He looked up through the tall grass. The sky was blue and spinning. He closed his eyes.

Doug heard a lone helicopter in the distance. It was making a rocket attack on Charlie's position. Doug flinched then hugged the ground as massive explosions devastated Charlie's front line.

As his head cleared, he focused on nineteen-year-old Sgt. Abrams standing next to him with an M-60 held firmly at his side. There were two extra belts of ammo strung across his shoulders. Doug knew that Abrams had killed the other two soldiers and probably saved his life.

Abrams grimaced through a mask of death and shouted as he moved. "Come on, I'm ready now, you motherfuckers. Come on, you slimy, slant-eyed cocksuckers!" Such offensive repetitions did not sound at all like Abrams.

Doug watched in disbelief as Abrams fired his weapon nonstop, ten-inch flames and white-hot metal erupting from the barrel. A savage death faced the dozen attacking soldiers and Abrams delivered it as fast as bullets could be sucked through the M-60.

Hunting frantically for his weapon, Doug searched the broken grass. The air was heavy with sulfur, hot lead and spent brass shells. After finding it Doug reloaded to assist Abrams. His firing had already dropped most of the charging men but Doug added his fire to the fight. Together, they killed five more of the attackers.

Doug stood about a foot behind Abrams and three feet to his right. When no one was left in Abrams' sights, he went slowly to his knees.

All firing had stopped. Twenty dead, broken, tortured bodies were scattered in the weeds and brush ahead of them. Doug knew that Sgt. Abrams had killed most of them.

Finally, Abrams relaxed and lowered the barrel of his weapon. A moment later he slumped forward. His weight and the momentum of his fall caused the barrel to dig deeply into the soft dirt. He was silent and still. His hand slipped off of the trigger and into the mud.

As Doug watched, he knew Sgt. Abrams was dead.

Catherine interrupted Doug's memories and spoke without looking at him. "What are we going to do, Doug? I'm really scared!"

"I don't know. I'm scared too!"

She did not respond.

After several more miles, Doug realized he was driving aimlessly and was almost at the Airport exit. The sun was gone and Catherine was unable to offer anymore help. He made a U-turn at the next off-ramp.

At least now they were heading toward home. Catherine lowered her seat and closed her eyes to sleep.

He thought about what needed to be done next. Once he was over the immediate shock of nearly dying, he knew they had to think much clearer about their next move.

His sense of being totally helpless was not as overpowering. Although those horrible sights at the hospital washed in and out of his mind like ocean tides, he was recovering.

Doug worried about Catherine but the more he thought about her the more he tried to convince himself that there was no real need to worry. She was upset and that was quite understandable but she would be fine after a while.

He knew she was emotionally strong, stable and thoroughly able to handle this shit. He remembered she was upset like this when her parents died two years ago in a plane crash. She and Kely both cried regularly for several months but they were able to go on with their lives right away.

The three of them had even gone out to dinner that very evening. There were weepy moments but dinner went pretty smooth considering the circumstances.

Doug touched her lightly. "Catherine, you awake?"

"Sure, I'm just thinking. What do you want?"

"I was thinking about stopping by the house to get the rest of my clothes. This will be the last trip until we get this situation under control. What do you think?"

"I don't know about that, Doug. Do you really think we'll be safe going there?"

"We can drive by first just to check it out and if it looks suspicious, we won't stop."

"Okay but first let's get a bite to eat." She added.

"That's an even better idea. Any suggestions?"

"Some place new, where nobody will recognize us."

"Any particular kind of food?"

"No, whatever you happen to see along the street."

They drove another five minutes and then turned off the freeway and onto a surface street.

Doug almost shouted. "Hey, there's a middle-eastern restaurant. Is that okay?"

She agreed.

They ordered their food without talking to each other and did not say much during the entire meal. When Doug finished his entree, he ordered a cold beer.

Catherine had not finished eating so he spoke first. "Are you feeling any better now?"

She seemed unsure. "Yeah, a little."

"As long as I don't over do it good food always helps me during times like this"

"Me, too." She stared into her food.

Doug kept the conversation going. "What did you think of this style of hummus?"

"It was different but I liked it. What about you?"

"I liked it too. It tasted better than what I make."

"That's what I thought but didn't want to say it that way. I think you need more lemon juice in yours."

He added through a smile. "Sounds like you're returning to your old self."

"Watch it, buster! And just who are you calling old?"

They laughed. Doug knew she was over the worse part of the trauma and that things were returning to normal.

She continued. "I don't know exactly how but somehow I feel we'll survive all of this."

"I think so too. It could easily get just as rough again but we'll handle it, right?"

She spoke with her usual enthusiasm. "You betcha!"

Doug changed the subject. "At my house we'll look up a pistol range in the yellow pages, then I'll teach you the basics of shooting. By the way there's a paper bag in the back seat of the car. It has the .38 caliber pistol I brought for you. It looked like the perfect size for your hands."

When she was ready to go, Doug took another gulp of beer and left the rest sitting on the table. They left hurriedly for the car. She went right for the bag and the gun. She pulled it out and looked at it, then asked. "Is it loaded?"

"Of course!"

She said. "Okay, tell me what to do with it?"

He showed her the safety and described how it worked. He told her that to fire at someone, just aim and pull the trigger. He put it back on safe when she was done looking it over. She asked several more questions and then put the gun into her purse when she was satisfied that she could operate it the way Doug would.

Doug stopped the car and parked around the corner from his house. They got out of the car to check out the situation from a distance. He took the .45 from under the seat and stuck it into his belt. Catherine checked the .38 in her purse and took the safety off.

They walked hand in hand, checking for activity on the street. At the corner they both just stopped and stared.

What a shocker, Doug's house was gone! *Those sons-of-bitches burned my house. They burned it to the ground, even the chimney had fallen. My two-story house is just gone.*

Their hands separated. Catherine continued to stare, not moving an inch.

Will this shit ever end? Doug walked toward the debris.

She whispered. "Wait a minute, Doug. Do you think it's really safe?"

Ignoring her, he continued walking at a faster pace.

She followed but with a warning. "Doug, be careful!"

Doug hesitated but looked up and down the street. There was no one in sight. The street was dark. There were many shadowed areas. He could not see most of them very well.

He slipped his hand inside the jacket. It brushed across the rough handle of the .45 and found the safety. He clicked it to the off position and pulled back the hammer so the gun would be ready to fire. Doug knew a bullet was already chambered. He slid a sweaty hand around the handle.

He was ready!

Tony had spent most of the afternoon in the LA County Recorder's office. It was now dark but he did not care. The file rooms were his personal sanctuaries when it came to finding someone for a client. He bragged that he could find information about any one living in the county if he was given enough time.

Usually all Tony needed was a person's full name, Dante Frederico de Casale and from there it was a piece of cake. He did not think that finding Mr. C would be as easy as it was. The trail should have been covered a little better.

Mobsters seldom used their real names when buying property, especially for themselves. So, he looked for an attorney connected to Mr. de Casale's name in some manner or another. That was the hard part since he did not know how deep it might be buried but at 4:30 p.m. he found it.

There it was! An entire law firm working solely for the mob. Every one of their clients was associated in some way with underworld activities. What a nice stroke of luck, he thought, then he shuttered at the prospects of knowing too much. It would invite a permanent stretch of extremely bad luck if the mob knew what he had just found.

He hated those mixed feelings. He wanted everything to be uncomplicated. For him they should be either hot or cold. He wanted no in-betweens in his life because they screwed things up too much.

An hour later he had Mr. C's street address. What a tangled mess of records, he thought. Mr. C should be in jail just for messing up the county's books so bad.

On his way to verify the address, he decided to call Doug with the good news. He also planned to brag a little about earning two grand in half a day. When there was only an answering machine with a woman's voice, he decided not to leave a message because he could not be sure who was on the other end to get it.

Instead, he called Dianna's home, giving her the address. To maintain the cloak and dagger atmosphere with her, he asked that she contact Doug at Catherine's number if anything happened to him. To build more melodrama he apologized for whispering and then suddenly excused himself.

Next Tony drove cautiously into Mr. C's neighborhood but stayed clear of Mr. C's street. Every street was lined with expensive, very fancy estates. Each of them probably had servants, gardeners and fancy maids, he thought.

Darkness covered the narrow streets. The streetlights of this well-groomed neighborhood were small, old and mostly ineffective. The homes were set away from the street. Thick stone fences and heavy metal gates were common and proclaimed the value of privacy and safety for the wealthy.

Some house numbers were painted on mailboxes but not nearly enough. Tony shuddered to think that he might be forced to leave his car to verify the address he sought.

Slowly, he turned onto Applegate Lane. This was where he would find Mr. C's address.

His heart pounded but he did not need its elevated rhythm to know how much he was scared. Just being this close to Mr. C's world was more than enough. According to his street locator, this one was only four blocks long. Mr. C's home should be in the second block and fourteen-forty would be in the middle and on the right side of the street.

His car inched slowly forward. He swore because he could not see most of the street numbers. He stopped at the end of the first block and turned off the radio.

He took a deep breath as the car moved forward again. He thought about turning the headlights off but reconsidered since that would make things worse if anyone saw him casing this pricey neighborhood. Finally, he decided to drive past the houses at a normal speed. That way it would seem less obvious to onlookers.

He accelerated to twenty-five miles per hour, looking repeatedly to the right and then to the left. Again he swore at the darkness. He drove well into the third block before stopping. He turned around and drove back to the middle of the fourteen hundred block where he decided to just get it over with as quickly as possible.

He stopped the car and opened his door. He walked over to the edge of the driveway. There it was on the wall, Fourteen-forty Applegate Lane. That was Mr. C's home.

He scanned the area through the silence. Nothing was notable. He turned to walk toward the open door of his car.

Someone shouted. "Hey, what are you doing?"

Tony jumped, turned toward the wall and spoke to the unseen voice. "Excuse me but I'm lost! I just wanted to check-out the number on the wall to get my bearings."

"Are you still lost?"

"Yes, I am but I'll just be on my way."

A chill sliced the night air as the voice ordered. "Not so fast, buddy! We already saw you drive by once."

Tony's heart jumped to his throat. This was exactly what he had hoped to avoid. His heart raced. His mind searched for options that would keep him alive. None were obvious.

His body felt like running. After all, the car's door was still open. He wished that little light inside the car was not glaring brightly at him like a childish tattletale.

Now his mind raced at full speed. *What should I do?* The only reasonable option seemed to be getting away from there by running for his life. He hoped he could make it. It was only fifteen feet so he ran!

Two shots rang out, sharp cracks in the still night, then silence. The shooter was very good at his job. Both bullets hit squarely in the middle of Tony's back. He was dead before his body tumbled into the front seat of his car.

Catherine and Doug had visited Fred Johnson's living room several times before tonight. He and Sally had been Doug's next-door neighbors for more than ten years.

Doug liked them both.

This visit was a half-hour old. Sally had served tea while Fred talked about the fire and how it had burned Doug's house. He recalled that it started around three o'clock in the afternoon. At first someone reported the smell of gasoline in the area but nothing about it was reported on the evening news. Fred swore that he had smelled it himself.

The fire units arrived in eight minutes but by then there was little hope of saving the house. Fred expressed concern that more had not been done for Doug since the firefighters spent most of their time just keeping the fire from spreading to adjacent homes. The water pressure of the fire hoses had broken two of Fred's upstairs windows.

Fred and Sally both offered to let Doug bunk with them for a while in a spare bedroom but he declined, thanking them for their long-time friendship.

Doug excused himself to get the address of a local pistol range from the yellow pages of the phone book while Catherine was being entertained. He was surprised that it stayed open until ten o'clock but knew many businesses never closed in Los Angeles.

Shortly afterwards, they said goodbye and left for the pistol range. It was 8:05 p.m.

Catherine was excited. She had never shot a gun before but claimed she had always wanted to. It was too bad that her wish was finally granted under such deadly circumstances. She insisted on taking a few shots to warm-up before Doug began her formal instructions. She allowed him only to show her how to hold the gun and how to sight correctly and that was it. She wanted to shoot on her own.

Her goggles and ear protectors were in place. The target was at twenty-five feet. Without hesitation, she popped off two rounds and then four more in rapid succession.

Doug could see that she had hit the target twice. He did not comment as she reeled it in.

"Oh, no! I was sure I did better than that."

There was a small hole in the silhouette's right shoulder and one in the area where a mouth would have been.

"Almost got him between the eyes, didn't I?" She bragged but her disappointment hung in the air.

Doug nodded in agreement.

"Okay. I'm ready for lessons, Mr. Sharpshooter!"

She removed her ear protectors.

Doug started the lesson. "Most people shoot too fast and that's the primary advantage a good shooter has over an enemy. The undisciplined combatant will lose the battle."

"Listen, Mr. Know-it-all. I don't have the slightest idea what you just said."

"It'll become clear in a minute. When you were shooting, each time you pulled the trigger, there was an explosion as the gun fired. Right?"

"Sure."

"Well that explosion has recoil associated with it, a small jerk when the gun sort of jumps in your hand, remember?"

"Okay, I'm still with you."

"Most shooters overreact to the jerk and that's the problem! They don't have what's called *good fire discipline*."

"That went over my head. What does overreacting and fire discipline have to do with it?"

"Fire discipline is what controls that overreaction. Do you remember the famous saying, 'Don't shoot till you see the white's of their eyes'?"

"Yes."

"Well, that was a form of fire discipline. Waiting to shoot until you have your best shot at the enemy!"

"That's easy. The closer they are, the easier they are to hit. That's it, right?"

"Yes but that's only a part of what's called acquiring the target. The Marines have a way of remembering how to maintain their own fire discipline. It's a very simple word that none of them have ever forgotten."

"What is it?"

"B-R-A-S-S. Breathe, relax, aim, slack, squeeze. You see once you've acquired your target, that's only half of the show. Then you've got to discharge your weapon, firing that bullet at the enemy in the most efficient manner possible."

"This is much too complicated, Doug. Are you doing this to me on purpose?"

"I know it's complicated but the stakes are high as well. If you don't have more control of your weapon than your enemy, then you'll be the one who dies."

"I understand that but I don't see how this helps me to shoot any better."

"Well, remember that little bit of recoil. With practice using B-R-A-S-S as a reminder helps to avoid that overreaction for most shooters."

"So how do most people overreact?"

"Finally we get to the bottom line question! They jerk their weapon ever so slightly. As a shooter fires, they unconsciously compensate for the impending recoil. It's just a natural response to the jerk but it affects their aim severely often causing them to totally miss the target."

"Oh so this B-R-A-S-S thing prevents me from jerking the gun when I fire."

"That's it, Catherine. That's one of the secrets of the Marine sharpshooter."

"Can you show me how it works?"

With an unloaded weapon he let her watch close-up as he went through the sequence. *BREATHE*. Doug took a deep breath and held it for half a second. *RELAX*. He let it out slowly. His hands were already raised in a firing position. *AIM*. He sighted along the gun barrel to the target. Doug kept his eye and the gun aimed at the target. *SLACK*. He moved his finger on the trigger, pressing it only to remove any slack, then he mentioned that hair triggers did not have any slack. Finally, *SQUEEZE*. The rest of his finger movement was required to raise and release the hammer. The hammer's impact on the bullet would then be a surprise.

He turned to face her. "When shooters stop anticipating the recoil, they usually shoot much better."

After watching Doug demonstrate it several more times, she took the gun and reloaded it. With everything ready, she fired six more times. Each of her shots was slower this time and four were right on target. Two were only a half-inch apart and centered in the throat area.

Doug praised her.

She beamed a giant smile as thanks for his help.

She reloaded and did the same thing again, then again. Finally, she placed all six rounds in the target area. She was a natural at this, Doug thought. She might even shoot a little better than he did in those early days.

She emptied the spent shells and handed the pistol to Doug. "Okay, Jarhead. Take your turn."

He took the gun and reloaded it. Breathe. Relax. Aim. Slack. Squeeze. It felt like a natural process to him so he pulled the trigger six times. The first one missed the silhouette by an inch but the rest hit the head area of the target.

He grinned as he handed the gun back to her.

She bragged for the both of them. "Watch out, Mr. C. We're deadly and we're coming for you!"

Chapter Eight

The street looked normal as they drove past Catherine's house checking for suspicious cars. She felt that everything was in its proper place and she recognized each of the cars on the street. After a second pass they felt safe enough to pull into the driveway.

Doug opened the garage door and pulled his Mustang inside, aligning it next to her car. She walked down the driveway to the sidewalk and checked the mailbox. Doug kept a watchful eye on the street since she was so exposed. He closed the door when she returned.

It was 10:30 p.m. *This has been a strange day.* Doug felt beat-up and exhausted. He had received a month's worth of negative emotional energy crammed into a few short hours.

He was ready for sleep, to dream and to get his mind focused on something more pleasant but he could not sleep, not just yet. First Catherine would pack and then they would drive to the safe house recommended by Agent Townsen.

Catherine started gathering the things she needed, placing them frantically into two sports bags laid across her bed.

Doug watched the street from a darkened upstairs window. This game had turned much too serious for him to not take all possible precautions.

He yelled to Catherine who was packing in the room across the hallway. "How's it going?"

"I won't be much longer!" She shouted.

A car stopped across the street. Doug's attention focused on the vehicle. It was a dark color, mid-to-large size. Because of the trees he could not see all of it but when the lights went off and no one got out of it, he started to worry.

The car was partially hidden in the shadows and it was impossible to recognize the occupants.

He called for Catherine to see if she recognized it as a regular. She did not. Since it did not belong there, they darkened the house and watched in silence.

Doug ran to the garage and brought back the shotgun with a full box of shells. He loaded it and checked the handguns, making sure they were each ready to fire.

They both moved downstairs to get a better view of the passengers. Catherine squinted, claiming it helped her to see a little better but still she could not identify anyone.

Then someone in the car lit a match.

For a brief moment while a young man puffed to light a cigarette, they saw faces in the vehicle. It looked as if all three were young men. After seeing them Catherine was now positive. She had never seen any of them in the neighborhood before that night. They were all strangers to her.

As Doug worried over the scene, his grip tightened on the .45 hanging at his side. He had had enough of this shit earlier in the day.

Catherine moved closer, whispering that she was frightened. He put an arm around her shoulder and squeezed but failed to admit that he was too.

The telephone rang.

They both stood frozen with surprised faces. They stared at each other as it rang again.

She whispered. "Should I answer it?"

"I don't know. It makes sense that Mr. C would have one

of his guys phone us while another one is watching the house so we can't easily escape."

Catherine crossed the room heading for the phone. It rang again. Each ring sounded louder than the last one. She reached for the telephone.

Doug glanced out of the window as the rear door of the car opened and someone got out.

He cautioned. "Wait!"

Her hand stopped as it touched the receiver.

Doug continued. "It looks like someone's getting out of the back seat and he's carrying a dark bag."

The telephone blared again.

A young man ran up the sidewalk to the house across the street and the car drove away.

"Looks like that kid lives across the street. He opened the door and went inside. Some of his friends must have dropped him off." Doug's anxiety eased.

Catherine jerked at the handset. "Hello."

It was a man's voice. "Is this Catherine Walker?"

"Yes, who's calling please?"

"This is Agent Townsen of the FBI LA Crime Unit. Is Mr. Carlson there?"

She covered the receiver with her hand. "Do you know an Agent Townsen?"

"Yes, that's the agent I mentioned to you earlier."

She held the telephone out to Doug as he walked across the room and took it.

"Hello."

Catherine moved to the window and watched the street.

"Are you two okay?"

"Yes. What do you want, Townsen?"

"I'm just trying to keep tabs on you. Our guys lost track of you when you left that pistol range."

"Are you trying to build up my confidence in the skill of your people?"

"Don't be a wise ass, Carlson! I called your house first and there was no answer."

Doug could not control his anger. "That's because I don't have a fucking phone anymore. It's melted into the heap of ash that used to be my home. Those motherfuckers burned it down this afternoon."

Townsen's voice was softer but still firm. "Take it easy. I'm sorry. I didn't know about that."

"So much for your fucking protection!"

"Well, you're alive. That's worth something, isn't it?"

Doug was not satisfied. "Yeah but little thanks to you."

"Look, I had eight of my people at the hospital keeping an eye on you this afternoon. I even had snipers on the roof so back off, Mister!"

"Okay. Okay. So that was you who saved our ass this afternoon."

"You're not planning to stay at Ms. Walker's house tonight, are you?"

"No. She's just getting a few things together."

"Well, there's no problem with that but get out of there as soon as you can."

"Sure."

"Also take her car when you leave. They might recognize yours by now."

"We can do that. Anything else?"

"Yes, are you going to the Paradise Motel?"

"We're planning to."

"When you get there, pump your brakes three times as a signal for Agent Wilson to bring you a cell phone."

"Is that really necessary?"

"It is! I want you in contact with me at all times. I want no more surprises, Mr. Carlson! Keep it with you at all times. That's an order."

"Okay, just until this is over."

"Mr. Carlson, try to get Ms. Walker out of town for a few days." He hung up.

The Pacific Coast Highway had always been a pleasant drive for Doug. The ocean was so pretty and alluring. With Catherine driving he would enjoy it even more this time.

He treasured such moments, a dark, clear sky, thousands of stars and a brightly-lit moon. The quivering reflections from the ocean surface were ever changing, moving, pulsing and throbbing, yet somehow, quite constant during his whole life. The scene was alive with complexity, yet projecting simplicity as an ideal image. Even the hell of Vietnam had this kind of beauty too.

"Catherine, do you want to hear a Vietnam story?"

"Sure if it's not too gory."

"It's not." Doug collected his thoughts.

"I was on a routine patrol. We had been in the field for two days and had just cleared a tiny Vietnamese village on the coast about thirty clicks north of the Chu Lai Marine Air Base. You know, I can't remember the name of it now."

Driving in the moonlight, Catherine's eyes were on the road but her thoughts were consumed by Doug's words. This was the first war story he had ever shared with her.

"There were only eight grass, tin and cardboard huts. The people were so poor they could not afford to waste anything.

They even used our garbage if we didn't bury it while they weren't looking. They had several fire pits used to cook for maybe two dozen people."

She felt anxious for his safety. "Was the enemy nearby?"

"There were no VC in the immediate area."

"What's VC?"

"That's what we called the Viet Cong, another word for Vietnamese Communist. Sometimes they were called Victor Charlie or just Charlie."

"Oh, was Charlie around?"

"Not among these peasants. Except for several women, there was only the very young and very old. Everyone else had left years before and was either dead and buried or still fighting somewhere else!

"We camped for the night on a grassy, tree-covered cliff overlooking the South China Sea. It was a no-moon night with only the darkness to conceal fleeting shadows. As we turned-in, three guards were posted. Mine would be the two to four a.m. watch."

"Was it scary. You know, with the enemy everywhere, all around you?"

"No, not that day. While I was on duty everything was quiet. When the breeze was just right I could hear the surf whispering as it pounded the rocks far below the cliff's edge. It was hard to stay awake so I yawned a lot. Eventually I had to stand and walk around just to keep my eyes open. I paced back and forth as the yawns continued."

She giggled but remained silent.

"Around 0330 I saw it, far out over the cliffs to the east. It was growing as big as a mountain. I knew I would never forget that morning for the splendor it provided. I was being treated to a moonrise over the South China Sea.

"It was silvery like a ghost mountain rising from the sea. I watched as it grew larger, turning into a large silver-gray circle like a coin, traveling upwards through the heavens.

"Tomorrow's monsoon approached from the right side of the moon like an eerie shadow creeping over the glowing sea. It darkened both the sky and water. From past experience I knew it would arrive about breakfast.

"A reflected shaft of moonlight stole silently across the shimmering water to greet my weary homesick eyes. It was not as good as being home but for that moment I was transported away from sore stinging feet and aching muscles.

"Gone was the lack of sanitation and irregular showers. Gone was the ever-present stare of hollow, hopeless eyes from people who had waged war for over a generation. Gone was that lingering uneasiness that I would never go home, not while I was still alive.

"My dread, fear and daily anxiety were relieved for that fleeting moment. I knew I could keep my sanity in that hell for at least one more day."

Catherine's voice pulled Doug's thoughts into the present when she responded. "That's so beautiful, Doug. Why haven't you talked about those things before?"

"I just couldn't. There is so much other stuff to explain and I thought that would be too hard to do."

She sensed his reluctance and changed the subject. "Oh, there it is . . . up ahead, . . . there on the left, the Paradise Motel. That's it, right?" She pointed with her free hand.

Doug agreed and took one last look at the moon's reflection on the ocean. For him these brief moments provided a sense of being emotionally revitalized. It was like looking into the face of all Gods' creation.

Ah-ha, this situation is so clear! Why didn't I see it before? Mr. C imposes massive stress on me and I have two choices. Accept it and learn to live with it or impose my own stress back on him and shift the balance points to where it's more comfortable for me.

Catherine did not sense the relief Doug's sigh brought.

Except for sleepiness, he felt calmer and more alive.

The car slowed as it turned into the motel. *This is not a bad looking place, new three-story buildings on the beach. It looks like four-star accommodations to me.* Maybe, the Feds knew what they were doing after all. He did not see anybody and wondered where they might be hiding.

Catherine parked directly in front of the office door. A one-foot tall sign hung in the window, broadcasting *Vacancy* in green neon letters.

Doug saw two people sitting inside, a man and a woman but he could not see anyone behind the registration desk. They sat in the car for a moment, talking about what to do next. It looked safe enough but they decided to be cautious.

Each grabbed their gun.

Doug stuck the .45 into the waistband of his pants knowing that it would be hidden from view when his jacket was closed. Catherine wore a coat with ample pockets. With her hands out of sight, she gripped the gun in one of them and it was ready to fire.

As they walked through the door, the couple glanced toward them but made no movement. Doug scanned them closely as he walked toward the registration desk. Catherine followed him without speaking. Finally, he saw the manager sitting behind the desk. She looked up and smiled.

As they moved closer, she spoke in a pleasant voice. "How you folks doing tonight?"

Catherine appraised everything in the room through cat eyes. First checking out the couple and then staying focused on the empty parking lot.

Doug responded calmly. "Fine. Do you have anything with a kitchen? We'll be staying a couple of days."

"I've got two. Both overlook the ocean, one's on the ground, others' on the third floor. What's your preference?"

"We'll take the ground level one." It would provide a quick exit if needed.

The manager pushed a registration card in front of him and he started filling it out with a made-up name.

The woman continued to chat. "You folks on vacation?"

"Yes. We just drove up from San Diego." Next Doug concocted a phony street address.

"Long drive, isn't it?" She queried.

"Yeah, we're pooped and ready to turn-in so we can get an early start tomorrow."

"You sightseeing or visiting friends?"

Doug handed her a hundred-dollar bill. "Both, we'll be doing a little of each."

She handed him the key for room 109. "If there's any problem just dial zero. I'll pick it up here. Good night."

He turned to Catherine who indicated with a nod that she was ready. She walked out ahead of Doug moving toward the car. As they walked, both scoped out the parking lot.

No one was in sight, at least that they could see.

Catherine drove about a hundred feet and stopped in front of the room. She turned off the engine. The radio continued playing soft music but she reached over and turned it off too, then she pressed the brake pedal three times.

They waited, looking in all directions. There was nothing, absolutely no movement at all.

Suddenly a light from slightly above them flashed on the car. Someone stood on a second floor landing about 30 feet away with a small hand-held flashlight. The person turned the light off and started walking toward the car.

Doug and Catherine both reached for their guns.

The figure, a man, walked down the stairs along the front of the building and approached from the left.

Catherine asked. "You recognize that guy?"

"No." Doug stroked the .45 with anxious fingers

The man stopped at Catherine's door and she rolled the window down a couple of inches.

Doug verified the safety on his .45 was off. He gripped the handle tighter and removed the slack in the trigger.

The man asked. "Mr. Carlson?"

Catherine replied. "Yes."

The man leaned over and looked inside. "I'm Agent Wilson. You folks alright?"

Catherine responded. "We're fine."

"I'm supposed to give you a cell phone to stay in contact with Chief Townsen. Have you ever used one of these before?" He displayed it at the window.

Catherine rolled the window down further. "Yes."

He handed it to her. "It has a special long-life battery and should last for about a week. You both have Townsen's personal number, right?"

Catherine turned to Doug and he answered. "Yes."

"And you have his access code too?"

Doug answered again. "Yes."

"If there's any shooting around here, let us do it. Do you both have weapons?"

Catherine responded. "Yes."

"Good. Stay out of sight as much as you can. Keep down and shoot only if someone's actually in the room and trying to kill you. Got it!"

"Yes."

"HQ's in room 216. Do not go there under any circumstances. Use the telephone to call us if you need help. We'll
come running as fast as we can. Any questions?"

Again Catherine looked toward Doug. He shook his head
and she responded. "No."

Briefly Agent Wilson stood beside the car, looked
around the parking lot then walked toward the office.

Catherine handed the cellular phone to Doug. "I believe
this is for you, my dear."

Catherine stepped out of the shower just as Doug finished unloading the car. She stood five or six inches shorter
than he did. She had a trim figure and worked hard to keep it
that way. Some jogging but for as long as she had known
Doug, she had taken aerobic classes. In addition, she used
most of the machines at her health club. She had earned her
nice figure through years of regular exercise with Kely.

Resting on the bed, Doug occasionally glimpsed her na-
kedness through the open bathroom door. There was just the
right amount of fat on her in exactly the places where he
thought it ought to be.

Since the motel was protected, it might turn out to be
their home until this mess was cleaned up. Doug had put
their luggage in the closet and even hung Catherine's clothing. The bag of guns was hidden there too.

When the bathroom was clear, Doug took a shower. He
enjoyed plenty of hot water believing that was what made a
shower great. He really needed this one.

By the time he was finished, Catherine had donned her
nightgown, the cherry colored one that was sheer but still

somewhat modest. She kidded him that she had chosen it because it kept her warm when she slept alone.

It was a few minutes after midnight.

Doug stood in front of the mirror with a towel around his waist, brushing his hair when Catherine walked in.

Standing beside him, she spoke. "Will we have to kill anybody or can the Feds handle it before that happens?"

"I don't know!"

"Doug, what did it feel like when you killed those guys last Tuesday night?"

"I haven't had much time to think about it. It happened so fast. All I remember is that I was plenty scared when they barged into my room."

"I'm scared just thinking about it."

"Me too! If the time ever comes to take action, you'll forget about being scared."

"So you just forget about your knees knocking."

He snickered then smiled at her comment. "Yeah."

"Was it that way when you were in Vietnam?"

"Well, not at first. The anticipation was the hardest part, not knowing when it might happen was tough."

"That's always the toughest part for me too. As a little girl, I could never go to sleep on Christmas or my birthday until I was simply exhausted. And Kely was the same way."

"Well, I think this is a bit different."

"I know but it's the same for me in those ways."

"I know."

They walked into the bedroom and sat on the bed.

Catherine gathered her strength and asked. "Doug, what was it like the first time you had to kill somebody?"

He looked at her in amazement. He had never talked

about that to anyone else, ever. Not even to his Marine buddies who were there when it happened.

She sensed his unsettled feelings then added. "It's okay if you don't want to say anything about it."

Doug swallowed and said. "Oh, . . . uh, I don't . . . uh, really mind talking about it."

"Well, you looked like you just grabbed the wrong apple in a pile and the rest of them came tumbling to the floor. Are you really sure?"

"It'll be okay. After more than twenty years it's probably about time!"

"Well, only if you're comfortable with it."

Doug took a deep breath and paused to think about how to get started, then began telling the story.

"I had been in Vietnam for five to six weeks. Several of my buddies would also get their first kill that day. A dozen of us were on patrol. We were in the jungle and had stopped to rest near a large opening in the trees. Charlie just happened to be on the other side of the clearing and luckily for us he entered it first.

"The Lieutenant ordered us all spread out, hiding about five feet into the treeline. When Charlie was about twenty feet away, we opened fire. There were ten of them and none of them ever saw what hit them. It was over so fast that none were able to even fire a single return shot at us."

She gasped.

"The one I had in my sights was also hit by someone else. Both bullets seemed to hit in rapid succession. This young soldier jerked wildly several times before he hit the ground. Afterwards I couldn't take my eyes off him.

"I was fixated on him even after he was dead, lying there broken on the ground. The closer I got to him, the stronger those feelings became.

"Somehow, I saw myself laying there! It was actually my body instead of his and it made me sick for the rest of the day. I wanted to run to that body and save it because it was really me. I had to save myself from being dead.

"Later as I walked past the body, I saw his eyes were still open. I won't ever forget the look on his face. That man was dead and I had caused it!

"Some of the others made a big deal, bragging about finally getting a first kill. You know that kind of stuff but I didn't. I couldn't. I never did anything like that."

"So what did you do?"

"Nothing. I pretended like it simply hadn't happened. I refused to talk about it. This is the first time anyone's ever asked me about it since that day."

"Oh, I'm sorry, Doug. I didn't know."

She got a beer from the fridge and handed it to him. She already had one for herself and had been drinking it.

"It's okay. A lot of time has passed since then. It's just that my first kill felt so different for me than it did for the rest of my Marine buddies."

She looked puzzled. "What do you mean?"

"Some of them seemed to enjoy it."

"Doug, they were immature, young men. They probably didn't have any idea of what else to think."

"Well, after that first time I never killed anyone except in combat situations. Everybody I saw through my sights was also drawing a bead on me and they expected it. That was war and in the heat of battle, they tried to kill me too. That's what made it different."

"That first guy was also a soldier so what was different about him?"

"He wasn't aiming at anybody and especially not at me. In another time and place we could have been friends with him dropping-by on a Saturday afternoon for a cold beer. I know that sounds crazy but it just wasn't the same."

"That's a pretty fine distinction, isn't it, Doug?"

"Yes but no one not even our enemies, deserves to die just for having a gun in their hand, unless he's also trying to kill someone with it. Does that make sense, Catherine?"

"Yes but that's not the typical image most people have of Marines, nor of their attitude toward death. Isn't it more like kill or be killed?"

"Probably and it was like that for me then but that's not the case today. Sure I killed a number of men on the battlefield but that was simply to survive, to save my own ass and I never did it again like that first time."

"Does that still bother you?"

"Not really, . . . well, yeah, I guess it does . . . I think about it sometimes. That was something I had to do then to just stay alive."

"Okay, take Mr. C for example. He probably will not have a gun in his hand but he's the one responsible for this. How would you handle him?"

"That's an interesting idea. He plans and directs everything but does nothing to me when we're face to face."

She countered. "That's right. He doesn't pull the trigger himself. Instead he hires goons to do it which causes other people to die, meaning that he pulled the trigger indirectly."

He knew what she wanted to hear so he said it. "Sounds like he deserves to die right along with his goons."

"It sounds that way to me too!"

Doug excused himself and walked into the bathroom. When he returned Catherine was already in bed with the sheet pulled-up to her neck. He could not tell whether she still wore her red gown or not.

She smiled as he turned off the lights and tossed his towel toward the dressing area. Doug slid into bed with his back toward her, tired and ready for sleep.

She moved closer, pressing her breasts into his back. They set him afire so he rolled over to face her.

The next morning Doug awoke at 8:10. There was no loud alarm and no bright-eyed DJ in the shower. There was only the slightest of movement from Catherine that just happened to brush him, not disturbing him but only bringing together his sleep awareness.

Doug felt relaxed. He opened his eyes and gazed toward Catherine. Hers were still closed. She lay on her stomach with her head facing him; hair draped across her face and nose. The sheet barely covered her naked bottom. One leg was uncovered and hung off the edge of the bed. Her skin was soft and smooth and brought pleasure to his eyes.

His hand reached for her. He stroked soft skin on her back, down to her waist and then up the curve to her bottom. He pushed the sheet aside. He cupped a round cheek in his hand and squeezed gently. He kept his hand on her bottom.

She made no signs of waking.

He stroked her head brushing auburn locks aside. Her face had soft, smooth features considered pretty to most people, even other women. On close inspection, faint signs of aging were there but not for most to see.

His heart swelled for her almost to the point of bursting. He loved Catherine. Sure he had not always shown it but he did. Of course there were other times he felt such feelings. Wanting to be with her but not actually making a commitment. She deserved that much from him but he could not.

He stroked her back moving upwards stopping on her shoulder. Tufts of dark hair had again fallen across her eyes and face partially hiding them. He blew lightly into it. She did not move. He blew again. There was still no response.

Her lips moved ever so slightly then flowed uncontrollably into her wonderfully wide smile. She tried desperately but without success to hide it from him.

Her pretense of sleep had been discovered so she turned her face away to hide the smile.

Playing with her, Doug whispered. "You can't hide now. I know you're awake!"

Suddenly she came alive, rolling toward him with a pillow in one hand. They struggled as arms and legs magically intermingled. She laughed with delight. They rolled around the bed and into a joyful morning.

A car door slammed in the parking lot and Doug jolted awake! He grabbed his gun and ran to the window peering outside. *What a relief!*

It was the couple next door loading their car to continue their vacation. Mom had just placed her toddler in his car seat. Dad was behind the wheel ready to hit the road. Once mom was finished and seated, the car drove away.

The parking lot was mostly clear. It looked like a nice sunny day. Doug headed for the bathroom and closed the door quietly behind him. After a few minutes, he noticed the door moving slowly.

Catherine was awake, opening the door just a crack as she peeked around the edge.

He whispered. "Looks like we've got a prowler."

In a made-up tough-guy voice she replied. "There's no one here, Mister. Your imagination is out of control. None of this is really happening."

Gruffly he responded. "Doesn't look that way to me."

She opened the door wider and through a pouty expression, complained. "Hey, can't a girl ever have any fun?"

Still pretending Doug said. "Oh, it's you! I was getting pretty scared."

"Yeah, right. I don't believe anything scares you, Doug."

"Well, how about that? It's not even ten o'clock and you've already made your first mistake of the day."

Using her tough-guy imitation, she ordered. "Listen up, Jarhead. I don't like being picked on especially by the likes of you before I even get dressed."

For a second Doug thought about what she had said and it surprised him. During the past few years they had found so many fun ways to play together. It had become an essential part of his happiness. He wondered if it was that way for her. *Is it that way for everybody?*

He felt there was something quite profound and somehow necessary in all of it but after a moment of contemplation, he let it go.

She wanted to continue playing the new script but he changed her mind. They took a long, hot shower together.

As they pulled into the restaurant's parking lot, Doug saw the Feds' white van following them. It drove past them and parked further down the block. It was nice to know they were out there if they were needed.

Catherine continued her playfulness during breakfast, maybe only covering up a growing anxiety but it was clear when she got serious. "Doug. Do you think we'll see those guys today?"

He knew the loaded .38 was in her coat pocket. A full

box of shells was in her other pocket. Her coat was positioned on the seat next to her for quick and easy access to the pockets. He wanted her to be ready.

Feeling anxiety Doug spoke. "I certainly hope not." His .45 was ready but he was not.

He secretly hoped that everything would somehow magically end. There had already been enough killing for him. He sighed. *Too bad, it's only a game for Mr. C.*

Responding to his sigh, Catherine leaned forward. "Are you okay?"

"Yeah. I'm really scared but I'm also afraid for you!"

"I know. I'm scared for both of us too."

With firmness he spoke. "Catherine, this is some dangerous shit we've got going."

Quickly she knew where he was headed. "Doug, I'm staying so don't even bring it up!"

"I'm proud of you for wanting to help me with this but it's just too dangerous."

"I'm not in this for your pride, Doug. I want to be with you no matter what happens. End of discussion!"

Frustration was taking over as he spoke. "I want . . . .."

She blasted at him. "Look, Doug. If somebody kills you, God damn it, I want to be there to shoot back at the fucker; I want to try and kill them even if they kill me too!"

"And that's exactly what might happen!"

Her passion grew. "Well, I'm ready to die right now if that's the way it's going to be." A tear flowed down one of her cheeks. "I'm not thrilled about getting hurt and possibly dying but I'm not running either, just like you."

She wiped her cheek with the back of her hand and continued. "Doug, I'm happy with our life. It's a good one and I will not let that son-of-a-bitch take it away from me without one hell of a fight."

"Okay but I hope it doesn't come to that." He knew she was staying regardless of what he might say.

She concluded. "Me too!"

They finished eating breakfast and sat for a while planning what they would do for the rest of the day.

The cellular telephone in Doug's pocket rang. *It must be Townsen; after all it's his phone.* He fumbled with it at first, finally getting it ready to speak.

He answered it.

"This is Agent Townsen. What the Sam-Hill are the two of you doing?"

"We're watching a movie. What's the matter with that?"

"You're supposed to be on the street helping us to find those mob characters who are, excuse me, hunting for you."

"What do you mean by that? The mob is busting their ass to kill us. I'm trying to stay out of their way until a better option comes along."

Townsen remained calm. "I thought we were working together on this and you decide to go to a matinee."

"Look. It's you who is looking for them and I'm willing to help but I don't know what's going on with your people."

There was no hesitation. "Okay. Here's the latest news."

Townsen paused briefly then continued. "Informants tell us the mob is scouring Ms. Walker's neighborhood for signs of your car. Once they find it, I suppose they'll figure you to be somewhere nearby."

"That's comforting."

"So here's my plan. Stop by Ms. Walker's house this afternoon and park your car on the street for them to find, then get the hell away from there!"

"Just what do you have in mind after that?"

"I plan to secretly clear out the nearby neighbors then we'll just wait for a hit later tonight. My team will take out all the bad guys except one. We'll let him escape and then follow him back to his boss."

"That all sounds pretty shitty to me. Catherine gets her house shot-up or maybe burned down like mine, just so you can track down this psycho."

"Look, since you can't deliver an address of this guy that pretty much limits your voice for selecting the options."

"Okay, have it your way!"

"Remember. Get in quickly and get out since timing is everything. Make it short and sweet, right?"

"I hear you. We'll do it as fast as possible."

"Good luck!" He hung up the telephone without waiting for Doug's response.

Catherine's car turned the corner onto Maple Street at 3:30 p.m. She wanted to get their part done quickly and then get the hell away from there in a hurry letting the Feds do their thing. Earlier she mentioned that compared to their lives, the house did not mean shit to her. She could always get another house when this was all over.

Doug agreed with her.

They both looked carefully down the street. Catherine felt that everything was in its usual place. Doug could not really tell but it looked okay to him. Slowly she drove forward; stopping directly across the street from her house.

She opened the garage door using her remote.

Quickly, Doug ran into the garage. Through the kitchen door he heard Catherine's telephone ringing. Taking an extra second he ran inside and answered it.

"Hello."

It was a woman's voice. "Is this Doug Carlson?"

"Yes."

"This is Tony Miller's friend, Dianna. Remember, I met you in the park yesterday?"

"Yeah, what's Tony up to now?"

"Didn't you hear the news this morning? Tony's dead. Someone killed him last night"

Doug gasped. "What happened?"

"I don't know but they found his body down at the dock this morning. He had been shot twice in the back."

"God damn! I was afraid of . . .."

She interrupted. "Hold on a minute. He called me last night with a message for you."

"What'd he say?"

"He just gave me an address, fourteen-forty Applegate Lane. He said you'd know what to do with it."

"I do."

They spoke another ten seconds and then said goodbye. Doug hung up the telephone and wrote the address on a nearby yellow sticky note pad.

Strangely, this activity excited him. It also scared the shit out of him. He stuck the pad of paper into his pocket.

Running to the garage he got into his car and backed it quickly to the street then jumped out and locked the door.

He glanced toward Catherine. She waited with the engine still running. She was ready to go.

He heard the sound of glass breaking from the house immediately to the left of Catherine's. Before he could react a shot rang out and the bullet crashed through his windshield, impacting somewhere inside of the car. Then there was a second shot, then a third and a forth.

Doug dropped to the ground as a bullet tore into the rear door of Catherine's car.

A moment earlier she had responded by stomping the accelerator. The bullet hitting her car was probably aimed at her and her acceleration had probably saved her life.

The car screeched down the street leaving behind the smell of burning rubber. *At least she's out of danger.*

Another half-dozen bullets ripped into the front of Doug's car before he had the .45 out and ready to fire. He stretched out on the ground looking around the front wheel.

He could see the broken windowpanes where the shots had come from. No one was visible but bullets kept pouring through the window toward him and the car.

The radiator exploded. Steam poured from the grill of the Mustang. Hot water rushed to the gutter. Doug felt the heat on his forearms.

From the number of shots it seemed there was more than one shooter in the house.

Doug extended the .45 around the front of the car's tire and squeezed off four shots.

He saw part of the wooden window frame shatter from the impact of his bullets. He jerked backwards as several bullets hit the ground in front of him.

Inching forward, he fired several more shots. Every one of his shots went straight through the window and the firing from the house stopped.

He raised his head over the fender but jerked it back down again as a single bullet crashed into the hood of the car. He loaded the pistol with a fresh clip and started refilling the partially used one with loose shells from his pocket.

He knew that automatic pistols had to be fed properly and often in a firefight.

There were no more shots. He prayed for it to be over.

Slowly he looked around the front tire. He did not see anyone but suddenly a burst of automatic rifle fire hit the ground in front of the car.

High-powered shells ripped into the asphalt throwing debris into his face and over the front of the car. There was a second burst of ten rounds, then a third longer one.

He peeked. Two men ran from the front door toward the car parked in the driveway and one of them was Mario.

Doug leaned forward and emptied the clip at the two men, hitting both of them. One man fell beside the driveway but Mario tumbled onto the hood of the car.

Quickly Doug pressed the clip release and inserted the waiting clip into the grip of the .45. In the distance, he heard the sound of squealing tires.

As he watched, Mario had climbed behind the wheel. A second man struggled to get the passenger door open.

Catherine stood hard on the brakes as her car shot past Doug. It skidded to a full stop at the end of her driveway. Instantly she threw open the driver's door and stood facing the fleeing men.

Doug yelled for her to get down but she did not respond.

Instead she raised her .38 to shoulder height, extended her arms and began shooting.

Two shots broke the momentary silence. The closest man dropped his weapon and fell to the ground.

Mario had the car running; he threw it into reverse and floored it. A cloud of black smoke poured off burning rubber; the car flew backward down the driveway and then screamed into the street.

Catherine fired at Mario even as his car moved toward her. Her shots were slow and calculated.

Doug saw glass fly around Mario as a bullet hit the passenger's window, shattering it; another one ripped loudly into the windshield post.

Mario slammed on the brakes as the car jumped the curb across the street and stopped diagonally on the lawn.

Catherine fired directly at Mario and made her best shot.

Doug saw that Mario was hit again because he dropped his pistol. Catherine fired again, hitting the frame between the doors. Sparks flew from the impact.

Catherine's bravery and her willingness to face-off with these thugs in a head-on battle stunned Doug.

After stomping the accelerator again Mario's engine whined loudly but there was no movement. He had failed to properly engaged the gears; instead getting it in neutral.

For Doug the scene appeared to freeze in time.

Mario stared at Doug, then Catherine. He looked anxious and scared. He leaned forward, fumbling with something on the front seat. Picking up an Uzi, Mario aimed at Catherine.

Doug raised his gun and aimed at Mario but a burst from the Uzi erupted before he could shoot. The Uzi did not require much accuracy; one only had to spray the target and would usually hit everything in sight.

Catherine's windshield exploded from the massive onslaught of dozens of bullets.

Doug saw her body jerk and fall out of view. He knew she was hit by at least some of those bullets and probably by the flying glass.

She did not scream as she fell.

Time returned to its normal cadence.

Hurriedly, Doug emptied his .45 into Mario's car hitting

its metal body in several places. If Mario was hit again, it was not apparent.

Mario fired another burst from the Uzi, peppering the asphalt in front of the red Mustang before he drove away at a high rate of speed.

Doug rushed around the car to Catherine's side.

She still clutched the .38 in her hand. He laid his .45 on the pavement beside her. The front of her white blouse was drenched in blood.

He pulled her several feet away from the car. His hands searched her torso locating two bullet wounds.

One was in her chest just below her left breast and another was in her left shoulder. The red, thick liquid flowed rapidly. A puddle began forming around them in the street.

She still had a pulse but Doug knew from his Vietnam days that she was quickly dying. Every drop of blood that flowed took her one step closer to death.

He sat on the pavement next to her and pulled her onto his lap. With his left arm around her to apply direct pressure to her chest wound, he tried desperately to plug the small hole and slow her loss of blood.

With his other hand, he fumbled in his shirt pocket for Townsen's cellular phone.

He felt her warmth as his clothes absorbed her blood. A wide stream of Catherine's blood flowed down the street and into the gutter.

Already sensing her impending death, he whispered to his love. "Catherine, please don't die!"

Tears flowed uncontrollably down his face. Holding her body close, with bloody fingers he dialed 9-1-1.

Chapter Nine

Two police officers waited in the emergency room for Catherine's arrival and stood guard around her throughout the rest of the evening. They were summoned by the hospital while the ambulance was still in route. Once she had been identified, the attendant expressed concern and called ahead for additional protection since no one wanted to see a repeat of yesterday's bloody shoot-out.

Doug called Kely directly from the scene minutes before the ambulance arrived. She was not home but he left a message telling her what had happened. Later he called again to give her the address where Catherine had been taken.

To Doug everything that happened in the Emergency Room seemed like it was straight from a madhouse, a form of unorchestrated emotional confusion. *How could anything ever get done in a place as upsetting and angry as this?*

Someone noticed Doug was leaving bloody tracks with his every step. A nurse pulled him aside and complained about the blood that covered his clothes and feet. She summoned a Red Cross Auxiliary volunteer who brought him a change of clothes. After changing and cleaning his shoes he went back to Catherine's side.

He was surprised to discover there were three other gunshot victims already being treated. Having witnessed what Mario had done, he could not contain himself. Anxiously he moved around the emergency room checking out each one.

He kept his hand out of sight but on the handle of the

concealed .45 stuck in his belt. Doug was taking no more chances. Luckily, none of them were Mario.

More than one person noticed that he was carrying a gun and eventually two doctors complained and refused to work around him while he had it but he refused to give it up.

They calmed down when a police officer insisted that Doug verify the gun was not loaded. He took out the clip and emptied the chamber but kept the unloaded .45 in his belt.

Doug stayed with Catherine during those early hours. At first, no one expected her to pull through or to ever have a normal life again but after a while her condition shifted from nearly hopeless to critical and then to stable although everyone agreed that she was still in very bad shape.

Doug knew she was lucky to have lived this long because of the river of blood she had lost. She transfused three pints of replacement blood before she was out of the Emergency Room. During the two and half-hours of surgery that followed, two additional pints were administered.

Her doctor voiced optimism about her condition and mentioned that since she was so healthy, her chances for survival were greatly improved.

One of her doctors mentioned that a bullet had barely missed her heart and it had done considerable damage to the surrounding area. While it did not injure the heart and was repaired quite easily, it needed to be monitored closely.

Kely arrived at 10:12. She looked as if she had come directly from work since she still wore a stylish business suit. Painful crying had already stained her lovely face and eyes.

As she rushed through the door, tears still streamed down her cheeks. She stood frozen, staring at Catherine's near lifeless body. Her hands covered her mouth, shielding an expression of horror and potential loss.

She looked hysterical but tried hard to control it. Doug was reminded of a similar reaction when their parents had died. Their family had suffered too much in a short period of time. He was relieved that she was not upset with him for Catherine's injuries.

Earlier Catherine had been moved from recovery into ICU. That was the first time anyone had told Doug that she might live and the doctor emphasized that his opinion was still very preliminary.

Catherine now slept quietly in a private room, affected by heavy medication.

A metal frame around her bed supported the plaster cast covering most of her left arm and shoulder. A dozen feet of breathing tubes were connected into a dense maze of artificial life-giving plastic that was then taped to her face and nose. She looked fragile and lifeless. Monitoring devices positioned around the bed, beeped and flashed regularly. An IV hung over her head connecting to her right arm.

The scene looked terrible and except for the continuous activity of various devices; it was one of death.

Looking at Catherine, Doug felt his heart rip apart. By now it had already been shattered into a hundred pieces. Seeing her lay there silently struggling to stay alive was almost too much for him to bear. Feeling Kely's outpouring of pain only deepened his tortured heart. His eyes welled and eventually tears streamed down his face too.

That should be me lying there instead of her. Even Vietnam was never as bad as this situation has become. At least that was war; this is nothing but nonsense! Nothing but a bunch of silly bullshit and it all belongs to Mr. C.

No matter how much Doug tried not to be involved, it seemed he has no choice but to protect himself. He thought about making Mr. C pay for all of this. He hoped to stay alive long enough to get even with him for allowing this to happen to Catherine and if he could not, Catherine would at least give it another try when she was able.

Kely moved closer and threw her arms around Doug. At first she just cried, sobbing wildly. Distress gripped and distorted her usually smiling, happy face. There seemed to be no end to the depths of her sorrow.

After countless minutes Doug wiped his eyes and offered a clean handkerchief to Kely. She took it, dried her tears and stuck it into her pocket. Doug knew she still needed it because each time she looked toward Catherine lying quietly on the bed, her tears erupted again.

The cellular phone rang. Doug took it and answered. "Hello, Agent Townsen."

"Good, you knew who it was. How's Ms. Walker?"

"She's out of surgery, stabilized and resting quietly."

"How about you? Are you okay too?"

"Yeah, just a couple of scrapes, minor cuts from all the broken glass. That kind of stuff."

"So, is she going to live?"

"It seems like it, at least for now. It's a bit too early for strong medical guarantees."

"I don't know if you've seen the news yet but the press is having a field day with this story out there. Every local TV channel is covering the shoot-out."

Puzzled Doug asked. "What do you mean?"

"One headline says, *LA woman takes on the mob and wins.* In another a TV newscaster is calling Ms. Walker, *The woman who stood-up to the mob.* Another says, *West LA woman clings to life after deadly shoot-out with the mob.* They're making quite a hero out of her."

This all sounded unbelievable to Doug but it did make

sense considering that the media would make a lot of money using lead stories like that.

"They've even got several of her neighbors talking live on the air as we speak. Nobody yet has said anything but fluff and feel-good stuff about her. It's all a bunch of sugar-coated stories about the nice girl-next-door.

"The woman who lives directly across the street is talking about actually watching Ms. Walker get shot. Saying that she returned home and began assisting you in your gun battle with the mob and that she killed two of the bad guys before they finally shot her."

There was a pause but when Doug did not respond, Townsen kept talking. "So, what actually happened?"

"They hid in the neighbor's house and waited for us."

"And there was no sign of them when you drove up?"

"No. We saw a car in the driveway but it was like the one that is usually parked there. Catherine thought it was safe so I moved my car. That's when the shooting started."

"The reports I've seen say that two of them died in the house and then the other two made a run for it. Is that basically the way it happened?"

"Pretty close. I have no idea how many of them were in the house. Once the shooting started, I was pinned behind my car most of the time."

Townsen added. "Those inside died of .45 caliber lead poisoning."

"That was me."

"So Ms. Walker had the .38."

"Right."

"That woman's a damn good shot. She put one bullet squarely in the man's throat and the other one through the edge of his heart. He definitely made a mistake tangling with her; he never had a chance."

Angered, Doug raised his voice. "And that fucker didn't deserve one, either! They . . .."

"I didn't mean it that way. She was such a good shot, he didn't have a chance of matching her shot for shot since he had already been hit." Hesitating for a second Townsen continued. "Say did you recognize any of those guys?"

"The man who got away is the one who shot Catherine. I remember him from Las Vegas. His name is Mario."

"That might be Mario Gallo. Was he tall and skinny with bushy, dark hair?"

Doug thought about it before he answered. "Yeah, tall and kind of thin."

"Sure does sound like him. Anything else?"

"No."

"Well, call me if you need help. I know we'll eventually get these guys out of your life."

Doug responded sarcastically. "Sure!"

"I hope Ms. Walker pulls through this." Townsen hung-up the telephone.

Moments after Doug started talking to Townsen, Kely moved to the edge of the bed and sat softly crying. When he hung-up the phone, she was holding Catherine's hand. The tears marking her face displayed deep sorrow.

She looked at him. "How did this happen, Doug?"

"Four guys started shooting at us from Mrs. Bryant's front windows. Catherine drove away at first but later came back when she thought I was in trouble. The story about the shoot-out is all over the news. They're talking about her courage for standing-up to the mob."

"What! You mean Catherine's on TV?"

"That's what I heard."

She stood up and placed her hands on Doug's upper arm and asked. "Are you okay, Doug?"

"Yeah, I'm fine." He held out one of his injured elbows.

She softly rubbed her fingers across his arm and the bandage. "You're both lucky this wasn't a lot worse."

Nodding, Doug agreed with her.

For a moment they gazed consolingly into each other's eyes; their cheeks brushed lightly during a comforting hug before their attention turned back to Catherine. Kely sat on the bed, taking her sister's hand again as Doug reached for the television and switched it on.

Doug turned onto Applegate Lane at 1:30 a.m. and it was just what he had expected. Mr. C lived in a very expensive neighborhood. *Wouldn't you just know it, a rich, irresponsible fuck! How many rich folks are concerned for their fellow man's well being? Did they ever want to do the right thing for others or just take care of themselves?*

It was around midnight when Kely had given him the keys to her car, telling him where she had parked it. The car was identical to Catherine's except it was green instead of white and was two months older. Not surprisingly, they owned many of the same things. A few of them were identical. *If one of these two women liked something, it was an even bet that the other one would eventually like it too!*

Earlier in the evening he had driven to the Paradise Motel and picked up their luggage with the bag of guns. Doug just felt like getting away from there so he threw everything into the trunk except for the black bag, which sat on the floor of the front seat. The shotgun lay on the seat next to him under one of Kely's coats.

He drove down the block at 25 miles per hour. He could not see very well because of the darkness and full-grown trees along the edge of the street.

The homes were set back from the curb with lots of bushes and other growth surrounding them. It was much too dark to read many of the numbers but he tried as much as he could. There were clusters of mailboxes along the street.

Driving down the next block, Doug saw a brick wall on the right that was much too high to see over. The rest of the landscape was much like the last block with trees, bushes and very little light to see much of anything else. In the next block, there was more of the same.

Doug realized that this was a very short street.

He was not surprised that Mr. C lived in an area like this since it was mostly hidden, secluded and very well protected from casual prying eyes.

He slowed at the end of the street as he turned the car around. With his headlights still on, he stopped the car and sat there just to think.

He had to figure this situation out before anyone one else died. *What should I do next?*

First, he would have to see everything on this street during the day when there was enough light to make a plan. He could not make a move until he had done that. The stakes were too deadly for any more carelessness.

Doug remembered being on that patrol in the Central Highlands of Vietnam. No one in his platoon took it seriously. Since they had seen no one during the first four days, they relaxed their guard just enough to get sloppy.

He recalled the unusual sight of ten Leathernecks playing around in the mountains while keeping only one eye out for Charlie. There was just enough horseplay for four of them to pay the ultimate price.

Hostile fire erupted from three different directions and

completely encircled them. At first they could not find the snipers who were well hidden in several clusters of trees and brush a hundred and fifty yards away.

The bright sunlight made the Marines easy targets and shooting back at the snipers was not easy since their concealment was so good. Their hiding positions even shielded their muzzle flashes and any rifle smoke when they fired.

Their first round of shots took down Corporal Jones and that new Private First Class (PFC). The second volley hit the Lieutenant but none of those early hits was life threatening.

There was no radio on the patrol so they could not call for help. Since it was a long-range patrol, there would be no one to pick them up or assist them until the tenth day if they made it safely to sector nine-four-two.

If they failed to get there on time, the choppers were ordered to leave without them. Everybody knew that was the rule so no one considered being late.

Luckily the snipers had not caught them in the open so it was not exactly an ambush. They found cover among a few rocks and some lame looking trees.

After ten minutes of not agreeing on the sniper's location, the Lieutenant sent four uninjured Marines to find and kill them. The first team scrambled to the south.

Doug led the second team to the north. He and PFC Hillman ran toward the ravine. Each carried an M-16 rifle and plenty of extra ammo.

Halfway to the ravine the snipers fired another round. It sounded like many more as the shots echoed across the hills. The bullets all hit the dirt around Doug's feet. He ran harder!

Several feet from the ravine, he dove into the four-foot crevice, preparing to crawl uphill from there. It was dry and rough. Hillman landed downhill from him but close enough for his elbows to impact the heel of Doug's boots.

Two more shots hit the dirt near Doug's head. Since there were only two, he thought maybe the third sniper could no longer see him. He crawled uphill frantically, moving forward as fast as possible.

Ten feet later, two more shots hit the ground somewhere behind him. He called out to Hillman who was okay but shouted that both bullets had barely missed him.

Doug continued crawling as fast as he could, much like a rodent in a newly flushed sewer pipe. In another thirty seconds, the firing was no longer directed at them.

He knew that they had moved out of the sniper's field of fire and that placed them out of their cross hairs.

He halted to look around.

Looking down the ravine, Doug could see the patrol scattered below in the rocks and brush about sixty to eighty feet away from them.

In rapid succession another round of shots filled the air. Unconsciously Doug measured the incoming sound to determine its source. It seemed to come from their right.

He moved hurriedly in that direction still going uphill but away from the ravine. He watched for action ahead as they moved. Hillman walked backwards a few steps behind him to cover the rear.

They moved slower now but that was the drill. In almost a squatting position, they waddled along the side of the hill. Their rifles were ready to fire at anything that moved. Since both of them were now in the open, making a wrong move meant that they could easily get wounded or killed.

On the next ridge Doug saw a small cluster of trees about twenty feet across. He stopped without signaling and Hillman bumped into him. They hit the deck then watched until the next round of shots shattered the midday air.

They agreed one of the shots had come from the trees on the next ridge. Finally, they had located one of the snipers. It would only be a matter of time until he was silenced.

Doug scoped out a cluster of rocks thirty feet uphill for a secure position from which to shoot. It offered better protection than just squatting in the open. They ran for it and positioned themselves among the rocks.

They waited for the next shot from the trees and when it rang out, both men sprayed the cluster with M-16 fire. They each fired thirty to forty rounds then stopped to listen.

During the next round of sniper fire, nothing seemed to come from the trees. They had done it! They had taken him out, well maybe. Now they had to confirm the kill.

Sixty yards ahead where the two hills met was a brush-covered ravine. Doug sprinted toward it while Hillman provided cover by firing into the silent trees.

In a matter of seconds, he jumped into the brush hoping no one had shot at him. Next Hillman moved forward as fast as he could while Doug provided cover for him.

The cluster of trees was now thirty yards away. The terrain was relatively smooth. They moved twenty-five feet apart in the ravine while staying hidden in the brush. They both inserted full clips of ammo into their M-16's.

As the next round of shots came, they charged the trees and made it into the brush surrounding them within seconds.

Doug entered the downhill side where there was a dozen trees around him. The thick undergrowth was two feet deep in some places. There were plenty of places for someone to hide but no one was in sight.

Hillman entered further uphill and immediately signaled that he could not see the sniper. Doug moved along the edge of the trees toward Hillman, checking out the brush with each step. He hoped it was clear along the edge.

He and Hillman moved uphill to the tree line. About ten feet apart they moved down through the trees and brush.

The sniper was probably dead by now but they had to make sure. Each step was torture, since they did not know if the sniper was still alive and at that moment had his sights trained on one of them.

They moved slowly, being as quiet as possible. After five feet there was no sign of trouble, then another five feet, still nothing. There had to be a dead body in here somewhere.

Doug signaled Hillman to halt. They both squatted for a moment to listen. There was no sound except for another round of distant shots from the two remaining snipers.

They stood and took several steps forward. There were no signs that a sniper had ever been there. Doug looked toward Hillman who was frozen in place. Hillman signaled that he saw something and pointed to the ground.

Nodding Doug moved closer. He moved silently, taking long, slow steps. Standing next to Hillman, he saw it too.

A covered firing position, a hole dug among the bushes. It was quite cleverly done and easily overlooked.

Doug signaled that they would each fire three shots into the hole from four feet away. When they fired, branches, twigs, dirt and other debris flew into the air. They stepped back a few feet and waited for a response.

The cover was damaged and bent but stayed securely in place. These VC are damn good builders, doing almost anything with only the most primitive of tools. Doug always said that they deserved more respect.

Hillman checked out the rest of the downhill area while staying clear of the hole. There were no other tunnels so the sniper had to be hiding in this one.

Doug sought a tree limb to raise the cover but nothing

was long enough so he improvised by connected their belts together with one of Hillman's bootlaces.

The makeshift rope was nearly ten feet long. He tied the bootlace to a fragmentation grenade, attaching it through the firing pin. Doug had created an unlikely looking weapon.

Hillman stood back protected by a small tree.

Doug tossed the grenade toward the cover, trying to get it to fall through one of the holes they had shot in it. It hit the ground past the hole and he dragged it slowly across the cover, hoping it would fall inside but it did not.

He tossed it again. This time it did fall through. He lowered it about a foot, then jerked, trying to dislodge the pin. It failed. He tried a second time but still with no luck.

Slowly he pulled, hoping that pressure from the weight of the cover would dislodge the pin. That failed so he pulled until the cover lifted slightly.

Three shots from an AK-47 tore through the hole. Now they knew the sniper was alive! The flimsy cover flew open as Doug jerked on the makeshift rope.

Hillman was ready. He had already pulled the pin on another grenade and without pausing, tossed it into the hole.

There was an immediate explosion, throwing dirt high into the air, tearing the cover off and sending it flying through the trees. Both men ducked and hit the deck. The belt rope was torn from Doug's hand.

When the dust cleared, they got to their feet and moved closer to inspect the open hole. It was four feet deep and then tunneled into the mountain. This kind of escape network was quite common for the VC. It gave Charlie an easy way to fire on them and then quickly disappear.

Doug tossed another grenade into the hole and dove into the brush for cover. The explosion sealed it.

The lights of an oncoming car startled Doug and dragged his thoughts back to the present. He was shaken by the idea that he might get caught in Mr. C's neighborhood with all those unregistered weapons in his car.

He had figured out what needed to be done but for now his first responsibility would be to reconnect with his once keen warrior mentality and recover his long-unused combat skills. They would be required to safely carry out his plans for Mr. C. He would have to start thinking again like he did when he was a Marine.

The lethal game Doug was caught in had turned into a private war with Mr. C. Once this sort of behavior would have been a piece of cake for him. He knew that he had to get all of that back again. *I just have too!*

He started the car, drove back down the short street and headed for the hospital.

Doug walked back into Catherine's room at 3:45 a.m. Her condition had not changed since he had left her earlier that evening.

Kely was asleep on the next bed. A blanket covered her to the waist. While sleeping, these two women looked a lot like twins; although they both assured him repeatedly that, they were not.

He went to Kely's bedside and touched her shoulder. She jumped and opened her eyes.

She barely spoke. "Oh, you're back. I figured you were gone for the whole night."

"No. I just picked up our things at the motel."

"There hasn't been any change in Katy's condition since you left. They came in to check on her a couple times but didn't say much to me."

Doug inquired. "Did you get any dinner?"

"No. They offered me a plate but I couldn't eat. With Katy just lying there."

"Are you feeling better now?"

"Yeah but I am a little hungry."

"Good. Let's go and get some breakfast. It'll clear up our heads a bit."

"No. I don't want to leave her, you know in case anything happens. I just don't want to be away from her."

"I'll go and get the nurse to check on Katy. If she's okay, can you leave just long enough to eat, okay?"

She hesitated but spoke. "Well, okay."

The nurse said Catherine was doing fine and everything looked good, adding that she would probably sleep at least until noon the next day.

As soon as Kely entered the front door of the restaurant, the first thing she did was to run for the bathroom. Doug knew she was deeply worried about Catherine; he was too. As she returned Doug spoke. "I'm sorry Katy got involved. I hoped she would keep her distance but she wouldn't."

Their food arrived at 4:30. The restaurant was empty and it still took thirty minutes to cook and serve them.

"I know. She told me all that Friday morning when we talked. You know that's exactly what she wanted, Doug."

"Did you hear there was a candlelight vigil outside the hospital last night for her?"

"No. Did you see it?"

"Yeah. It was going at midnight. About a hundred and fifty people were still left then."

"That's cool. How many were there all together?"

"The radio newscaster estimated about a thousand."

"I'm glad there are so many people praying for her."

"Me, too!"

"Was what they said about her on TV last night true?"

"Pretty much. All except that part about her tracking the mob for weeks. She didn't do any of that. Neither of us did. Some crackpot reporter just made it up."

"Sometimes they'll just say anything. Won't they?"

"Sure but they're not fooling anybody with it anymore. Today most people realize that only half of their dazzle and gore is really true."

"So, why do they still do it?"

"Come on, Kely. You know it makes money!"

"Right but I forget about it so easily."

"That's exactly what they rely on, people forgetting."

"What do you mean?"

"Most people don't remember after a few days. Of the few who do, only a couple of them will ever speak out, then it's easier to discredit them."

"Yeah. By making people look foolish most will probably keep quiet in the future."

"Exactly and after a while nobody speaks up."

"What are the police doing about all of this?"

"Not very much. It's considered a federal problem since the mob's involved. Every report goes straight to the Feds who have got a task force just to handle organized crime."

"So those policemen outside of her door are all the help she'll be getting from them?"

"It seems that way."

"Do you think they'll come after me too, Doug?"

"There's a good chance, Kely so don't think otherwise."

Her hands went to her face. "Oh, my God!"

Immediately, tears rolled from both eyes.

Doug decided to tell her the whole story. After what had happened, she at least deserved to know what to expect.

"Kely, I know where Mr. C lives and I'm going after that motherfucker tonight."

She gasped. "No, Doug. You can't. I don't want you to."

"I've got to. There's no other way out of it but I'll need some help."

"I can't do that kind of stuff, Doug. I'm not like Katy; I'll just get in your way."

"Oh no, I didn't mean you, Kely. There are others I can call to help me with new wheels. Then I'll check out his street and hopefully get in undetected. That's probably all I'll need help with."

"Do you really think you can do this?"

"I know I can!"

Her face seemed to change, then she asked. "Would Katy have done what you're asking?"

Pausing, he nodded, then responded. "Yeah, I think so."

Smiling much the same as her sister, she said. "Okay, count me in! Where do we start?"

"Well, first of all you need to . . .."

The blue van turned west onto Applegate Lane. It was a few minutes past 8:30 a.m. Kely drove slowly down the street keeping the speed at 30 miles per hour. A loaded pistol was hidden on the seat next to her.

Since she did not know how to shoot, it provided only emotional security for her. When she first heard the plan, she said. "Oh, I can do that!"

Doug sat in the second seat with a video camera pointed toward the window. His feet were on the seat and his knees supported his elbows. He recorded the scenery as they drove on Mr. C's street. He planned to do the same thing along the other side as they drove back.

The .45 lay on the seat between his feet.

He needed to have a good look at both sides of the road and this seemed to be the best way to do that without causing suspicion among the residents. A quick drive up one side of the street and back again should do the trick, then he could watch the tapes repeatedly in the safety of Kely's living room. That is, until he figured it out what to do next.

The van passed fourteen-forty and he felt strangely excited. He knew Mr. C's house was somewhere in these few blocks but he saw it first in the camera. *So that's where Mr. C lives.* His house was the one behind the brick wall. It looked to be the most protected one on the street. That was certainly no surprise to Doug.

Without moving, he spoke to Kely. "Tonight, I'll take the show to Mr. C. but this time I'll march right into his home probably scaring the shit out of him. I'll let him see who he's been fucking with."

Kely nodded, hoping that everything would really be as easy a Doug expected.

First, he needed to find a safe way over the wall and onto the property. Next, he needed to move around the grounds undetected. Because of the wall he could not see much of the terrain around the house.

Kely swung the van wide at the end of the street and completed the U-turn without hesitation. She set the speed of the van at thirty as she drove back along the street.

Doug kept his eye glued to the camera's viewer. Fortunately he only needed to do this once and he was sweating even that. Mostly he was afraid of somebody seeing them and then of Kely being shot like Catherine had been.

This reconnaissance reminded Doug of the time his patrol was caught in the middle of an enemy HQ meeting.

Six Marines had been inserted thirty miles south of the demilitarized one. They believed hostiles were in the area but had no idea about what to expect from Charlie.

It was only mid-afternoon but in less than two hours they were in the thick of it all. Their jobs had been to set-up and maintain a lookout-post for the next seven days. Within a couple hours they had found a suitable location.

There was lots of ground cover situated in a thick stand of trees. Occasional openings in the jungle canopy allowed the sun to shine through. There were changes in elevation but mostly it was flat.

Two men were stationed high in the trees with portable radios. They were about fifty feet in the air but neither could be seen from the ground.

The base and radio were hidden under a large downed tree that had fallen several years earlier and was now mostly deadwood. Several others had fallen onto it so the buildup of brush and creepers offered a good deal of concealment.

While the radioman was verifying his equipment connections, two PFCs accompanied Doug to check out the surroundings and place additional equipment.

There was an open area about fifty feet across and thirty feet to the south. Five trails lead into the opening from every direction. This should have tipped them off to potential problems but at the time no one noticed.

They installed experimental and still secret motion sensors along the trail a hundred and fifty yards from the base. Three more sensors were placed where the brush was less dense, just in case they later became paths. This network of sensors completely encircled the base.

The last sensor was in place only twenty minutes when

someone activated it. They were all so busy setting up that only one of the treetop lookouts actually saw the intruders.

Four North Vietnamese Army (NVA) soldiers were advancing into the area. They scouted cautiously along the trail. Their point man moved forward ten feet at a time, then stopped to listen. When he felt it was clear, he motioned for the others to advance; it was a slow process but a safe one.

Three of the Marines were positioned near the base to protect it. Wearing green and black face paint they blended quite well into the brush and tall grass. There was great concealment but very little cover.

Their weapons were locked and loaded. If a fight came, the Marines were ready for it.

Eventually the NVA patrol arrived in the clearing where they halted and cautiously inspected its perimeter. One of them came within three feet of Doug but did not notice him. After completing their inspection they relaxed their guard. Next they separated with each soldier checking out one of the remaining paths and returning to the clearing about five minutes later.

PFC Holms, the radioman, quietly sent a message about the enemy patrol while the others maintained their guard. Each Marine was ready to open fire at the first hostile action from Charlie. Fortunately none occurred.

There was no opportunity to move to more secure positions. In a half-hour there were at least fifty NVA soldiers milling around in the clearing. *It was almost a full house and still they kept coming in groups of two or three.*

Holms later mentioned that every one of the sensors had been tripped multiple times. That meant Charlie had arrived from every direction of the compass. *It was too bad the sensors were unable to count them as they passed.*

The lookouts in the trees tried to count them all but lost

track or gave up when the count exceeded two hundred. *That was one hell of a staff meeting!*

Two NVA soldiers sat only five feet from Doug with their backs toward him. One of them slept as the other listened to the commander, a captain, major or something like that since Doug could not determine his actual rank.

As part of their celebration, they passed around dozens of bottles of gook jungle-brew and everybody, except the Marines, had far too much alcohol to drink.

A brushy area near the tree where PFC Jones was hidden became their urinal. He swore that each man pissed on the bushes at least four times that evening. It was soggy and smelly all over the area and especially where he sat. He was sick for hours afterwards from the intense smell.

Finally just as they had arrived, they faded into the night. By nine o'clock, the clearing was empty. Not a single shot had been fired. When the last NVA soldier was out of sight, the Marines ran for the bushes to empty their own bladders.

The listening post was operational for another week; the men in the trees moved further out so they could count the traffic on the trail better. Doug smiled at his recollection of that mission because no one had to die on either side.

Kely interrupted Doug's thoughts as she spoke. "What do you think? Was that good?"

The van turned off of Applegate Lane

Realizing where he was, Doug shut off the camera before responding. "Oh, uh, . . . yes. You did fine, Kely. I think it was perfect!"

"I got scared when that limousine approached. Did you see where it turned in?"

"No."

"It went into fourteen-forty. That's Mr. C's place, right?"

"Right."

"I wonder what that means?"

"I don't know. Maybe, Mr. C's decided he needs help."

Chapter Ten

Kely's funny-bone was roused when she first glimpsed Doug dressed all in black; to her he looked like one of those cartoon ninja characters she had seen on TV. His black and green face paint added the final touch. She giggled about it the whole time he was getting ready.

He did feel strange dressing like that but that was how it had to be. He knew it would be difficult enough getting into Mr. C's estate undetected even with this kind of camouflage and he would probably not complete his mission without it.

He was not going to underestimate Mr. C ever again.

Doug was pleased. Kely's attitude was more like Catherine's than he had expected. It was give 'em hell, Doug and I'll help if I can.

Earlier Doug stopped at a surplus store and bought the things he needed--four used holsters, several webbed belts plus miscellaneous items. He saw lots of other neat stuff but bought only those to help him deal with Mr. C.

Kely reported that Catherine was about the same, critical but hanging-on like the good trooper she was. She had not awakened yet and Kely stayed with her most of the day, only leaving to drop Doug off at Mr. C's estate.

Catherine had become quite a celebrity. People from all over the hospital went by her room just to get a glimpse and to wish her well, although she was not awake.

Even the hospital administrator dropped-in to see her

while Kely was with her. Now the quality of her care would be at the highest possible level. After all, everybody knows that celebrities and heroes deserve and usually get the best. Too bad Catherine was not awake to enjoy the attention.

Doug strapped on the holsters and placed a pistol in each one of them. Their fit was not as good as he wanted but they would do fine. He installed silencers on two of the pistols, which made them fit even more awkwardly.

The TEC-9 was placed in a custom designed holster he fashioned from a wire clothes hanger attached to one of the webbed belts. A flat shoulder bag bulged with hundreds of rounds of ammo and several extra clips. Kely had filled the clips for him but later he checked each for proper loading.

Kely gave him the penlight she carried in her purse on a key ring. It was extremely small but provided a powerful little beam of light. Finally, he stuck the sawed-off shotgun into one of the belts.

He inspected everything in the mirror. It did look funny but he was ready!

Doug spent the afternoon watching the tape he had made earlier. The street was narrow with just enough room for two marked lanes. Drainage ditches lined both sides within a foot of the paved surface and there was no place to park or stop a car on either side of the road.

It was just your basic rural layout without sidewalks and gutters, a unique situation to find within a major urban area like Los Angeles. There were no streetlights at all.

Actually no lights of any kind could be seen from the street. At night darkness was certainly a big safety factor for Mr. C. So if Doug did not take a light, there would be none.

He found a place where he planned to bale out of the van. It was a hundred and thirty feet from the corner of Mr. C's block near the western edge of his property.

There would be no reason for Kely to stop the van as long as she drove slow enough. Doug's departure from the van and getting to the bushes should take less than ten seconds. He would then go over the wall as the van drove back in front of Mr. C's estate.

That was where the easy part ended.

Kely stuck the key into the ignition of the van and Doug looked at his watch. It was 8:05 Saturday evening. Almost a week had passed since that first meeting with Mr. C in Las Vegas. Too much had happened since then.

Doug remembered that his watch beeped every quarter hour so he took it off and laid it on the front seat.

He also took the bulb out of the dome light so it would not light up when he opened the side door of the van. He tied a six-foot piece of cord to the handle so Kely could close it after he had jumped.

He cinched up the combat boots he bought that morning. He had not worn that kind of shoe for more than twenty years and he was surprised at how comfortable they were.

Kely spoke before starting the van. Concern filled her soft voice. "Doug, are you sure you want to do this?"

He was not turning back now. "I'm doing it so let's go!"

She backed out of her driveway and headed for the freeway. In twenty minutes she was nearing Mr. C's street.

Doug made one last check of things.

Everything seemed A-Okay as the van made the right turn onto Applegate Lane. The headlights lit up the road ahead of them but no one was on the street.

Kely adjusted her speed to exactly 25 miles per hour.

As she neared the jump location, she would let the van coast briefly. Hopefully, the speed would be slow enough for

Doug to jump and remain on his feet. To Kely the van seemed to barely crawl.

Doug watched dark shapes pass. He took a long breath and let it out slowly. He was ready. Twenty-five miles per hour seemed to be much too fast.

At the end of the first block he unlatched the sliding door but kept it closed. He sat on the floor out of sight.

He grabbed one of the guns with a silencer. He pulled it out and checked that it was ready to fire. He stuck it back into the holster with the safety on. If there were guards patrolling the grounds, it was for them.

It was almost time, another seventy-five feet.

The van moved forward. Doug knew it would not be much longer. Passing in front of the gate, he raised his head and peeked out of the window.

He did not see anyone or anything except the metal gate and that was a good sign.

At a hundred and twenty feet he raised up and fully slid the door open. He pulled on a pair of dark kid-leather gloves. He was ready to jump and hit the road running.

Kely raised her foot. The van coasted.

"Good luck." She whispered.

Doug stared and could not acknowledge her. He took another deep breath and held it. He was ready.

Near the edge of the brick wall, he leapt from the van as it slowed to ten miles per hour. Hitting the ground, he started running as quickly as he could.

He took five or six giant steps but they were not nearly enough. He fell to his right knee in the ditch, then lunged forward landing on outstretched hands and forearms. He rolled to his right shoulder and then onto his back.

His mind raced to determine that he was okay. Quickly,

he checked his gear. Everything was in its proper place. Each gun was secure; none had been lost.

He looked down the street toward the van. It was nearing the end of the block. The street was empty in the other direction. He stood, headed for the bushes at the property line and then to the corner of the wall.

Doug looked toward the street and waited.

Shortly the headlights of the van approached. He felt along the top edge of the wall. It was smooth. *What, there's no shards of glass or metal barbs? Come on, Mr. C you disappoint me. This is much too easy!* He was pleased since he was unable to view this part of the wall in the video.

The van moved closer.

Grasping the top of the wall, he waited for the van. As it passed, he jumped and pulled himself to the top of the wall. Doug rolled across it and in another second was on the other side, squatting on the ground.

He had done it. He was inside of Mr. C's estate. For several seconds he crouched and listened.

There was no sound to be heard. He pulled out the .38 with a silencer and clicked the safety off. The only lights he could see came from the house about seventy-five feet away. There were two other lights shining in the area around the garage.

He moved toward the front gate fifty feet away.

The sky was dark except for occasional stars. The moon had not yet risen. Doug was in the open but it did not matter since he was wearing dark clothing. Dressed all in black he knew he would be extremely hard for anyone to see.

He moved slowly and stopped every few feet to listen. Occasionally he glanced toward the house to verify that no one was moving there either. He was determined not to be surprised.

Suddenly, there was a burst of light ahead as somebody lit a cigarette. He covered his eyes.

Now there was no question about it. Someone was stationed at the gate someone who could not be seen from the street. It did not surprise him when he considered who lived at this secluded address.

Moving closer, he watched the glow of the cigarette and in a few seconds he smelled it. *How many battle deaths are caused when soldiers light up at times like this?*

As the man puffed, flashes of light illuminated another person standing next to him. They both stood near a small booth also hidden from the street. Doug wondered if there were more than the two he could see.

Doug was now twenty feet away.

He stayed close to the wall, creeping silently. They did not move around much but instead chatted softly. *On quiet streets like this one they were probably bored stiff.*

A car approached and one of the guards peeked around the fence, looking through the bars of the gate. Pulling his head back, he reported. "Looks like the Jefferson's."

Their chit-chat continued.

Inching forward, Doug was only ten feet away, hugging the wall. He felt like his Marine stealth skills were serving him effectively.

Waiting for the next car to drive-by took about ten more minutes. During that time the two men changed places several times as they took turns casually peering through the gate, mostly at nothing.

Doug saw light from an oncoming vehicle in the distance beyond the gate. That would be his signal to attack.

It did not matter to him who he shot first. He waited as the man closest to the gate stepped backwards, then turned to identify the vehicle.

Doug stepped away from the wall and raised the .38 to fire. He aimed carefully.

There were four muffled shots in rapid succession. He fired at the closest one first, then immediately shot the second man. He shot each one a second time before either one of them hit the ground.

He ran toward them, ready to shoot again if either had moved but they did not. Quickly he frisked each of them for concealed guns, which he tossed into the darkened area where he had hidden only seconds ago.

A rifle with a scope stood in a corner of the booth. He removed the clip and cleared the chamber, then tossed them out of sight in the shadows. Next, he dragged the bodies out of view and replaced the four spent shells in his .38.

The driveway curved slightly to the left before arriving at the house and garage. From the gate, trees and intervening shrubbery largely hid the house.

Doug ran thirty-five feet to the first row of shrubs. He stopped to look and listen. It was quiet. No one else was in sight. He breathed a sigh of relief.

He fought his way through the shrubs and positioned himself behind a large nearby tree. He could see the front of the house and part of the garage.

Everything was well lit. He waited and watched. The closest cover was forty feet to his right near the garage.

He stayed in the shadows moving around the yard but froze when a light on the side of the garage came to life.

He squatted in the shadows hoping that he had not been seen. A man walked from the back of the house along the side of the garage. He was being led by two dark colored guard dogs held tightly on leashes. They looked like Dobermans but he was unsure. As they reached the front of the house, the automatic light went off.

Doug stayed away from the garage but slowly moved around the house. He went as far as he could and stopped until he could figure out how to handle the roving sentry.

Four minutes later the light was activated again by the same guard and his dogs who had circled the house earlier. Doug knew how much that kind of guard duty sucked.

Still in the shadows but a bit closer, Doug waited.

One of the dogs pulled to the left looking toward him. He held his breath hoping the dog had not detected him.

The guard responded to the pull of the dog and stopped. Unfortunately, the second dog's sensitive nose quickly found the scent of the first.

Doug raised himself slightly and backed into the bushes. He was completely out of sight when the guard fanned his flashlight along the bushes. He shielded his eyes.

Still using the flashlight the guard pleaded. "Is that you, Joe . . . Abe? Come on, guys, I don't need this shit tonight!"

He leaned over and did something with the dogs.

In a heartbeat Doug recognized the guard's intended actions. *Oh, shit! He's removing their leashes.* He hated to shoot the dogs but they had been trained to kill without hesitation. Unfortunately, that was their job. Now Doug had to do his. He had to kill them.

Hurriedly Doug sought a more secure hiding place realizing it was probably too late for that now. The guard stood and the two dogs raced toward him.

These bushes would be of little help so he stretched out on the damp grass. Doug's arm supported the .38 in front of him. He was ready but not eager to shoot.

He watched as the dogs ran closer.

One of them pulled slightly ahead. When the first dog

was ten feet away, Doug pulled the trigger. The dog's frightened yelp drowned out the muffled sound of the silencer. A heartbeat later he killed the second dog.

Doug raised his eyes, looking across the grass toward the guard. Now, Doug had his attention too.

The guard reached for his pistol. Doug fired two quick shots. The guard fell backwards into the loose gravel. Doug held his breath waiting to see what would happen next.

Ten seconds later the light went out. He dragged the dogs to the bushes and reloaded the .38.

Turning his attention to the guard, Doug approached the body. As he walked within twenty-five feet of the garage, the light came back on.

Quickly checking both directions he picked up the man's gun, tossed it far into the grass, grabbed the man's arms and pulled him across the lawn into the bushes where he had hidden the dogs.

To calm down a bit, Doug waited for the lights to go out before daring to move. Staying near the garage, he moved further around the house where he noticed a small shed with its lights on. It was built adjacent to the garage and seemed to have only one door.

Moving closer, he expected to trip the automatic light and he did. Doug inched up to a window and peeked inside.

He saw a man sitting at a desk; a semiautomatic pistol laid in front of him; a radio played soft rock music; the volume was low. He was reading a paperback novel.

Doug moved around the shed to its door. Slowly he turned the knob determining that it was unlocked. He yanked the door open. The surprised man jumped to his feet. As he dropped his book, the man reached for his gun. Doug fired two shots into the man's chest.

The man crashed backwards across the chair, making a

loud noise as he hit the floor. Doug closed the door silently and ran into the shadows.

He waited to make sure no one would respond to the crash. After five minutes he relaxed thinking that no one else had heard the shooting.

It seemed strange that Mr. C had no surveillance equipment on his property. There had not been a single camera. Nothing was at the front gate except for that small booth and no monitors were in that guard shack behind the garage. Doug knew that Mr. C had the bucks; obviously, he was all bucks and no brains.

Remaining in the shadows Doug moved to the back of the house where many oak trees had been planted in a semi-circle around the patio. They were now mature and had grown together forming a solid wall along the back of the property, affording Mr. C lots of privacy.

The patio was very well lit. There were strings of lights, maybe fifty, strung across it and they were all on. The entire back of the house was lit up like a Christmas tree. Every window glowed from the inside.

Doug was surprised since the front of the house appeared so deserted. Yet, in the back it looked like a party in progress. The giant patio stretched from the house and meandered out and under most of the trees.

There was a pool in the distance with several changing rooms. This grand house was undoubtedly the pride of this wealthy neighborhood.

Maybe Mr. C's party had just moved inside. Doug's fears began to grow. Maybe there were women and children. Doug certainly hoped not.

If so that would be too bad. Doug knew he would have to be hard when dealing with Mr. C. Thinking about guests, Doug decided that if it were possible he would not shoot unless the person had a gun ready to use on him.

Doug thought about his rules of engagement so having a gun meant you died; that seemed fair. No matter what, he was completing this mission. He was nailing Mr. C's ass, come hell or high water.

He replaced the spent cartridges and ran toward the back of the house, where he stopped to listen.

The closest window was five feet away. Slowly, he moved to it. There were no sounds yet but he was bathed in light from all the glowing windows.

Doug took several more steps and stopped. He inched his way onto the wooden patio. A French door into the house was ten feet away. Soft curtains hid his view of the room.

Silently, he moved toward it; grasping the knob, he turned. *It's unlocked!*

Hesitating, he listened. There was silence. He opened the door a crack and peeked inside. It was empty.

He pushed against it. It opened wider, then a bit more until he confirmed no one was there. The room was empty. This was a lot easier than he thought it would be.

Doug reached into the holster grasping another silenced pistol, a semiautomatic. He held it firmly in his left hand. Stepping forward he moved cautiously into the room and pushed the door closed behind him.

Doug whispered to the empty room. "It's time, Mr. C. I'm here. Watch your ass, motherfucker!"

Chapter Eleven

Moving across the room to a second door, Doug opened it a crack and peeked through it. He saw a long hallway leading to the left then turning to the right. At the spot where it turned he saw two big burley guards.

They stood like statues next to the closed double doors. Dressed in crisp business suits, hands clasped in front of bulky bodies. They looked formidable with solemn faces.

It was quite a display. Clearly, they were guarding Mr. C but why such an effort to protect him from unwanted intrusions? *It looks important. What's Mr. C planning now?*

If Mr. C knew Doug was this close, he would be scouring every hiding place on the grounds and Doug would be dead as soon as the hired goons found him. But, Mr. C could never imagine him being inside of the house and this close to shooting his rotten sorry ass.

Mr. C's home was quite elegant. This room appeared to be only a sitting room but was furnished more grandly than the nicest room in Doug's burned home. Several big windows overlooked the patio and the doors multiple panes of glass added to the panoramic view of the patio. There was a comfortable cluster of sitting furniture arranged to one side. A small glass coffee table stood in the middle of the chairs.

Doug passed a mirror and noticed the concealing face paint he wore. Smiling at Kelly's earlier laughter, he took a moment to wipe it off on a nearby pillow.

Personal photos arrayed an entire wall. From the numbers it appeared that Mr. C was acquainted with many local influential people. Viewing the many smiles and embraces convinced Doug that he was well liked. Within his large circle of friends and acquaintances, Mr. C appeared to be a rock-solid, pillar of the community.

Doug knew that every group of people had a few who refuse to think for themselves, the bay gulls. The ones who failed to question anything around them and always go with the program, no matter what the personal cost.

He wondered how many of Mr. C's friends, the people in those photos, were like that? *Did any of them really know Mr. C? Did they know something that I might have missed? Had all of this shit just gotten out of hand?* It was too late for those kinds of questions.

For now it really did not matter to Doug. He did not care what others thought of the situation. It had become very simple for him. He was here to eliminate the threat of Mr. C and his goons and to avenge their shooting of Catherine.

It was nothing more than a preemptive strike to destroy their capability to hurt him or anyone else. Doug planned to defang this mad dog. That was it, plain and simple.

The guards stood like misplaced statues, neither moving even an inch. From only twenty-five feet away they looked straight ahead to where Doug hid but failed to see him.

Unless Doug thought of something soon, he would be stuck there hiding in Mr. C's home. If any of the dead bodies were found, all hell would break loose.

He scanned the room to come up with a plan. There was a bookcase with twenty or thirty books. A curiosity toy sat motionless on the coffee table. There were several cabinets along another wall and a nearby closet. A serving table with drawers and a couple of tables with large lamps, one had a pottery base, were placed around the room.

He wondered about that lamp, maybe it would break if he helped it a little. He went to the lamp and traced its cord down the table leg to the floor and under the chair to an area rug, which hid it from guests. He traced it to a wall plug.

Doug unplugged the cord and pulled it from underneath the rugs back to the lamp.

Moving back to the door, he peeked again at the two goons. Neither seemed to have batted an eye since he last saw them. They seemed to be frozen in place.

He held the lamp cord and pulled on it to tighten the slack. The .38 with the silencer was in his other hand.

He pulled on the cord trying to slide the lamp. It was so heavy that it failed to budge. He pulled harder and the lamp barely moved. He yanked it one final time.

The lamp crashed to the floor, making a noise so loud that Doug cringed. Instinctively he tossed the cord across the room but kept his eyes focused on the guards.

From the surprised looks on their faces he knew that both of them had heard it. They finally moved, looking somewhat puzzled at each other. Doug knew that something would happen now and he was ready for it.

The men in the hallway spoke softly. Doug could not hear what was said but one of them drew a pistol from under his jacket. It was a semiautomatic nine-millimeter.

He walked toward the door where Doug hid. Doug's heart raced as he closed the crack in the door and stepped to the corner of the room behind the door.

The door opened slowly but not enough to expose him.

Calmly the guard walked in without checking things out. He moved directly toward the shattered lamp with his back toward Doug.

Without hesitation Doug pulled the trigger twice shooting the guard in the back. There were two muffled sounds as he was thrown forward into the furniture. The guard pushed one of the chairs into a table, causing another lamp to fall, creating a similar crashing noise.

Doug heard the second man running down the hall. He pulled out the TEC-9 getting ready for a serious shootout.

A voice cried out. "What happening, Pete?"

Doug took a deep breath. He had been in situations like this before when the shit was getting ready to hit the fan. His mind reeled at the coming confrontation. Unwillingly he focused on a *search and destroy mission* back in Vietnam.

His squad was moving through a destroyed Vietnamese town that Charlie had seized a week earlier. Originally, there were dozens of brick buildings but after the fighting, it was hard to tell exactly how many there were.

Most other buildings were made of wood. One was the grand two-story French Hotel, *Le Lis Rouge*. The peasants' homes had been made of grass, cardboard and tin; they had already been burned and their inhabitants fled.

With sixty Marines advancing through the town and only ten percent of it secured there would be some serious fighting ahead. Charlie was dug-in very well. During the morning, he had resisted every Marine advance with expertise so the fighting had been heavy and bloody.

It seemed that Charlie was planning to stay a while but the brass had other ideas about where he could go.

The objective of Doug's squad was to secure the hotel. Cautiously eleven Marines moved forward between scattered debris and overturned vehicles. If Charlie was still inside, he held his fire. *Those sneaky bastards*!

There was little glass left in any of the windows. Several holes in the front wall demonstrated the massive damage that could be inflicted with heavy weapons.

As they prepared for the assault, several smoke grenades were tossed along the front of the building. When the cloud was dense enough to shield their movement, four Marines including Doug, ran for the front porch.

Charlie opened fire from inside the building. The transformation from sporadic shots cracking in the late morning air to repeated rapid burst of semiautomatic weapon's fire was instantaneous.

As expected, charging Marines dodged a hail of bullets. Dozens thumped into hard-packed dirt around Doug's feet as he ran. Seconds later they reached safety and scrambled for defensive positions across the porch.

Charlie punctuated his anger as shots blasted directly through the wall from soldiers on the other side. The porch was sprayed with bullets then it was quiet.

Doug noticed that the smoke had drifted away when the warmth of the tropical sun bathed his neck and legs. From his position he heard nothing more inside the building.

In a heartbeat PFC Avery lobbed a fragmentation grenade through a nearby window. Everyone hugged the wall as the explosion shook the entire porch. Debris shot from windows; smoke bellowed like a house on fire.

Doug held his breath.

Instantly Avery was up, jumping through the window as dust and smoke filled the air. Doug heard three bursts from his M-16 as he killed whoever was still inside. Avery stuck his head out, smiled and signaled that it was clear.

The rest of the Marines entered the ground floor.

The downstairs was a big gutted burned-out room. Two dozen dead bodies lay helter-skelter throughout the littered chamber; dozens more littered the stairways.

There was broken furniture among a layer of debris. Usable stairs stood at both ends of the giant parlor. A smashed counter sprawled at one end. Doug wondered if it was guest registration or a bar? Now it was impossible to tell.

Two Marines moved toward each staircase with M-16's at the ready. Doug heard footsteps as Charlie repositioned himself upstairs to prolong the battle.

Halfway up the stairs Doug heard a burst of gunfire from the other side of the building. Three bullets impacted the wall ahead of him.

He knew it was Avery since he usually shot first and then looked to see what he had hit. He was a damn fine Marine who had earned two Silver Stars just since Doug had known him and also three Purple Hearts.

Everyone knew that Avery took far too many risks. He claimed that since he had no one left at home, he could do what no other Marine had the balls to do. Usually that was exactly what he did.

Doug advanced to the top of the stairs. Quickly he stuck his head out to look around the corner.

Avery was already standing at the other end of the long hallway. Four dead bodies lay in front of him. Ten doors lined the hallway; some were open but most were closed.

Doug's thoughts caused him to shutter. Each door leading to a side room was a place for Charlie to hide. Before anyone could move Avery kicked-in the first door. Doug watched as Avery lunged through the door to his stomach.

There were no shots so it must have been empty. Avery reappeared and moved to the next one.

Systematically they checked each room. In minutes all were secured except for the one in the middle.

Without waiting Avery kicked at the door and dove into the room; it erupted with AK-47 rifle fire. Bullets tore into everything including the door and broken walls.

Charlie had apparently retreated to this room and Avery's ass was in deep fucking shit. Doug assessed the situation. Avery was on the floor. He had been hit but while lying on his side still fired his rifle.

To assist, Doug fired at the gooks across the room near Avery. Using short rifle bursts, he hit both of them. They were down but still alive. One stretched to reach his rifle; the other moved reflexively.

Several shots tore into the half-open door. *Shit, there's someone else in the room behind the fucking door.*

Doug leapt forward just as a burst of semiautomatic fire ripped the door in half. Showered with wood chips and debris, he hugged the floor. He moved and tried to fire but was grabbed by one of the men he had just shot.

With Doug and Avery both on the floor the Marines in the hallway fired directly through the walls, spraying the entire room.

Doug was being held securely by huge arms tightened firmly around his neck, like a giant snake; he was being strangled. That young soldier was considerably smaller than him but had the strength of a much bigger man.

Gasping for air, Doug watched as Avery fired at the men across the room behind the splintered door. Both had already been hit but neither was ready to stop fighting. Finally one of the other Marines burst into the room with his M-16's ablaze; in a instant he killed the last standing gook then sprayed a growing pile of bodies, killing the wounded ones.

As Doug gasped for air, another Marine kicked the soldier strangling him. A second kick to the man's face was necessary for him to relax his death grip on Doug.

Gasping, Doug rolled away from the soldier just as a blast of M-16 fire shredded the man's head.

Later the Lieutenant promoted Avery to Lance Corporal while scolding him for being too reckless, adding that if he was not more careful he would probably end up dead.

Avery's pained, cocky response echoed in Doug's mind. "They can only kill me once and after that the Nam can't hurt me anymore!"

Remembering Avery's words Doug bolted into the hallway to face the oncoming guard.

Pushing the door hard, it slammed into the wall with a crash. He knew the sound would get the attention of others but now he was ready for it all to finally happen.

As the guard ran toward the disturbance, his gun was drawn but not quite ready to fire. Doug was and fired two quick muffled shots.

The first one hit the guard's left shoulder. It did not stop him. The second one hit him in the face just above his right eye. Instinctively his eyes and mouth flew open from the surprise and destruction of his brain.

With a bullet in the brain he was probably dead or would be soon. He fell with a soft thud landing on his stomach.

Doug continued running toward the closed doors. He noticed an elegantly printed sign on the wall, *The Cabo Room*. He stopped several feet to the left of it and listened.

He heard men's voices and hoped they had not heard what had just happened to the guards. He moved close to the doors and placed his ear against it.

Two voices engaged in routine conversation. Doug could tell only that they were talking about money; it was something about a million dollars.

Doug thought about what he should to next. Should he look around the house for others or go in and finish the job quickly, here and now? He could not decide.

After a moments hesitation he thought about how this situation was similar to that patrol in Vietnam when that NVA staff meeting surrounded them and were in their rifle sights. Each Marine was in a good firing position. It had been an excellent time to kill most of those NVA soldiers. With two Marines able to shoot from the trees and with most of the NVA drunk, it would have been so easy. The NVA would have had a difficult time to even fire back at them. That would certainly have been one hell of an ambush.

Doug would have gotten more kills that night than most grunts did during the entire war. If any one of them had fired, that was how it would have happened.

Maybe Charlie would have killed a Marine or two but it would have been the biggest, most disorganized grab-ass session any of them had ever seen. The NVA would have been tripping all over themselves just to get out of the way. It would surely have been one fucking bloody mess.

It was okay with Doug the way it actually worked out. None of them had the nerve to stir-up that kind of serious shit. Maybe in some ways Doug was a bit smarter back then.

He raised his foot high on the double doors and kicked hard against them. They flew backwards into the room, crashing loudly. Both hit the wall hard enough to fully embed the knobs deep into the plaster.

Doug stepped into the room and shouted. "Don't anybody move. I want hands in the air. Now! All of them!" He motioned upwards with one of his guns.

The startled look on Mr. C's face was apparent to everyone in the room. They all looked at one another as they each stood up but no one spoke.

The room was large. A single long conference table was straight ahead next to the wall. To Doug's right was a nicely decorated bar with a south of the border motif. It looked to be as well stocked as any small bar he had ever visited in town. There were a dozen small round tables pushed to the left. Maybe thirty or so chairs were stacked in the corner.

Doug motioned for them to move from behind the table.

Following orders, Mr. C shouted his outrage. "What the fuck are you doing here, Carlson?"

"Oh, you're not very happy to see me? I thought for sure you would be."

"You're one dead motherfucker; you know that!"

"Come now, I'm sure you wanted me here. How many people have you sent to get me during the last few days?"

"I didn't want you here asshole. I wanted you dead."

Doug waved the TEC-9 at him. "Well, that's not very likely now because my buddy here sees things a bit different than you do."

"Okay, Carlson. What do you want?"

Doug raised the .38 to shoulder height and aimed it directly at Mr. C. "I want your ass, fucker and I want it now!"

"You'll never get away with anything like this."

"I think maybe I already have. The rest of your fucking goons are already dead; there's just the four of you left and now I'll finish the job I came here to do."

"Wait a minute! To get this far you must know how difficult it was to find me. I've got a lot of connections and you'll never be able to get away with this and live!"

"And why is that?"

"You think you've had big trouble with just my boys after you. Now there'll be a hundred guys after you at once. You won't be able to handle all of them. Not this time."

"I'll worry about them later. Once I take care of you everyone will think twice before fucking with me like you did."

"Killing me won't scare them one bit."

"Maybe not but getting at me has been a nightmare for you and it's going to get a lot more painful and expensive for anybody else who tries."

"That's no problem. My friends will pay that price."

Mario went upstairs to rest after finishing his dinner. He had slept for most of the day and now began to feel stiff.

The bullet wounds in his left shoulder had been cleaned and bandaged yesterday by old Doc Jacobs. The bandages on his cuts and scrapes made his injuries look worse than they actually were.

Feeling restless, Mario climbed out of bed and headed for the Cabo Room. He knew he could get a stiff drink there anytime of the day or night.

As he stood, he instinctively grabbed for his pistol.

Doug walked forward and stopped in the middle of the room. He holstered the handgun but kept the TEC-9 leveled at Mr. C and his cronies.

"We'll just see about that. I don't think you have friends dumb enough to follow your sorry, fat-ass tracks!"

"Hey, you watch your mouth, Mister!"

"When anybody with an ounce of sense hears how all this shit started, they'll forget about your chicken-shit ass and get back to their own business."

"Just keep talking, Mr. Wiseguy! Keep spouting your shit. There's nothing you can do to stop what I planned for you even if you shoot me!"

"If your friends are stupid enough to still come after me once they find out how you pissed away your entire organization over a spilled drink in the casino last week, then they deserve a big dose of the same shit."

In surprise several of the men turned to look at him.

Mr. C shouted defiantly. "You know this guy's crazy. That's not how it happened. He's just making up that shit as he goes along. Can't you tell he's lying?"

Suddenly everything went black for Doug. He remembered dropping the TEC-9 as his eyes closed and he fell to the hardwood floor.

Chapter Twelve

When Doug opened his eyes, he felt like he was back in Las Vegas on that sticky bloody bathroom floor. Again his face was covered with blood. He raised a hand to touch it, to feel it run down his cheek. He sought the cut on his face but did not find it. He found the lump on the back of his head. The pain was bearable.

It seemed that Mr. C got even with him while he was out cold. Kicking him when he could not feel it or fight back but he could feel it now.

Doug sat up and noticed the guns piled on the floor near the end of the bar. The shotgun lay on the table with shells scattered about it. The contents of his shoulder bag formed another pile. Mario sat at the table with his gun placed neatly in front of him. *That's probably what he used to hit me.*

Mario's face looked bad, like someone had beaten the shit out of him. With bandages on his head and face and his right arm in a sling he looked as if Catherine had done quite a number on him. Doug wondered what Mario had told Mr. C about the unfortunate encounter.

Mr. C held the TEC-9.

Leaning over Doug he stuck it in his face and yelled. "Looks like your plans fell through, Mr. Carlson, didn't they? Now, who's the asshole?"

Barely managing to move Doug stretched and squinted. He was still numb from the bump on his head. He tasted the blood in his mouth as it bled. He took a deep breath and spit into Mr. C's face, blood and all.

Mr. C jerked back in surprise and reached to cover his face. Frantically he wiped the mess with his sleeve.

Cradling the TEC-9, he began kicking wildly at his prey.

Doug curled into a ball. Mr. C's outrage was evident in the kicks but again the pain was bearable. After ten kicks, Mr. C was too tired to continue. He shouted for help to pick Doug up. Two nearby men grabbed him by his arms.

He barely stood on weak, wobbly knees. He leaned to the right and balanced his weight on one of the goons. Mr. C stood near the door several feet away.

He spoke to Doug. "So, Mr. Carlson. I want to know exactly how you found my house?"

"You don't really expect an answer, do you?"

His voice softened. "Sure, what's it matter now?"

"Well, fuck you anyhow!"

"Awe, don't be that way. We know it came from that dick we shot the other night. You did know him, right?"

"I don't know what the fuck you're talking about."

"Well, I think you do."

Suddenly there was the ring of a cellular phone in one of the goon's shirt pocket.

Mr. C yelled. "What the hell is that?"

It rang again. Doug's mind raced.

He knew he had to act quickly. Remembering how he had once done this, he tensed up both arms and jerked, rotating his body to the left.

The man on Doug's left lost his grip. The motion threw him forward toward Mr. C as Doug fell to the right into the other man who was pushed into a third.

All three then fell toward the bar. As the last man let go of Doug, he rolled toward the guns.

He saw Mario scrambling to get his gun. He heard the TEC-9 erupt as Mr. C tried to kill him by spraying the room. Someone yelled in pain as a shower of Mr. C's random bullets hit them.

Doug did not see who was hit but knew it was not him.

He grabbed a .45 as Mario fired a bullet into the bar next to his head. Continuing to roll Doug no longer saw Mr. C.

He stopped at the end of the bar with his back resting against the wall. He looked up and the phone rang again.

Mario was ready for another shot. He fired and the bullet hit the floor between Doug's legs. A third shot struck the wall next to his shoulder. Splinters flew around him.

Remembering what he had told Catherine about shooting, Doug took his time aiming.

He fired at Mario's chest and hit him. Mario fell backwards into the wall then slumped to the floor. Doug fired a second shot at him under the table. He saw Mario jerk from the second impact. He was dead.

Doug stood at the corner of the bar. The first man was only now getting to his feet. Doug saw him reach into his coat for a gun. He was ten feet away when Doug fired. The bullet struck him in the stomach. He doubled over and dropped the gun. Doug fired again as he fell to the floor.

Counting quickly, Doug knew there were only three of Mr. C's men remaining.

By now Mr. C had emptied the thirty round clip. In his rage he threw the gun across the room trying to hit Doug. It slammed into the wall behind the bar.

Mr. C rushed to the front of the bar. Doug fired as he ducked out of sight but missed, hitting the wall behind him.

Using another gun, Mr. C fired at Doug through the bar.

Doug knelt in front of the fridge. Its door flew open and hit him in the face as several bullets spent themselves inside of the heavily insulated appliance.

Leaping to the other end of the bar, Doug saw wood splintering around him. Bottles shattered to his left; bullets ripped the back wall apart.

He crawled along the back of the bar as Mr. C continued shooting into it from the other side. Shots continued until he emptied a fifteen round clip.

Doug peeked around the other end.

Another man was just now getting back to his feet. The third man was lying on his face with a pool of blood on the floor around him. Mr. C had killed one of his own people trying to get at Doug.

Mr. C still clutched the pistol in his hand but jerked it as though it was still firing.

When he saw Doug, he dropped it.

His face distorted in horror for what would surely happen next. Turning slightly he pressed against the bar like he was trying to hide. *What a chicken shit! After all this he's pretending to hide from me.*

The last man moved toward the table where the shotgun was laying. Fumbling, he picked it up and started loading it.

Doug stood and aimed at Mr. C. He stepped away from the bar and walked closer.

Mr. C looked at Doug with tears in his eyes. He held his hands toward Doug like he was praying.

When Doug was three feet away, Mr. C began crying like a little boy who had been caught doing something he knew he was not suppose to do.

Mr. C pleaded. "Oh, please, Mister. Don't hurt me any

more! I didn't mean anything by it. I was just playing. You can have everything back and I won't tell anybody about it either. Oh, come on, Mister. You know . . .."

Feeling disgust for his pathetic tears Doug fired the .45 twice. Mr. C flew backwards and slumped to the floor.

Glancing sideways Doug looked at the man standing at the table. He fumbled terribly with the shotgun as if he had no idea what he was doing.

Doug raised the .45 as the telephone rang again.

Noticing Doug, he stopped loading the shotgun, dropped it and then dropped the rest of the shells one by one through anxious fingers.

Waiting for the last one to fall Doug spoke. "Say good night, motherfucker!"

Despair flushed the man's face as he fell to his knees. Even in panic, he held his head proudly. Doug saw the fright and knew he was scared shitless.

His voice quivered as he spoke. "You don't know me, do you Mister and I don't know you? I have never done anything to you, have I?"

Doug paused then moved closer while keeping his gun pointed at the man's head. "I'm sorry but that stopped being important to me a long time ago."

"Listen. I've done a lot of bad shit in my life but I haven't ever killed anybody. I just never thought it was the right thing to do!"

"Can the bullshit! You've been doing this fucker's dirty work and that's enough for me to shoot your nuts off, right now asshole."

Shaking his head, the pleas continued. "No, that's not the way it is. This is only my second day here. You shot Mr. de Casale's boys up so bad last week he needed fresh ones. Everyone here's brand new. Mr. Gallo rounded us up yesterday straight from the streets."

Doug was pleased, surprised and suspicious. "Are you shitting me?"

He raised his hand as if to make an oath. "I swear, Mister. That's what happened. Look, I got a wife and three kids; it was just a job for me. Mr. Gallo offered me a grand a week and I need the money for my family. That's the only reason I'm here, honest."

Still unsure about the story Doug paused. He hoped there had been enough killing for one night.

He lowered the gun but kept it aimed. Doug moved around the room so he could talk to the man as they spoke and still watch the open door.

Doug spoke. "What's your name?"

The man stuttered. "Uh, . . . Marc Turner."

"So you're a married man with three little ones. What's the wife's name?"

Stammering again. he continued. "Lucy, uh . . . her name's Lucy Anne Turner."

Underneath his breath, Doug swore. *Motherfucker! Am I gonna fall for this lame, piece of shit story?* Doug asked. "If I put this gun down are you still going to try and shoot me?"

"No, uh . . . no, I won't. I promise I won't." He raised his right hand as if to swear again.

"Okay. Sit in that chair and don't move a fucking muscle, do you understand?"

"Yes, sir. I'll do exactly what you say. Lucy and I owe you a really big one, Mister."

Doug's pager had started vibrating right after he shot Mario. Now he reached into his shirt pocket and pulled it out. He did not recognize the number but he went to the telephone on the table and dialed it.

It was Kely at the hospital.

Her voice broke as she spoke. "Doug, . . . is that you, Doug?" She sobbed openly.

"Yes but why are you paging me at a time like this?"

"I don't know, Doug. I just had to talk to someone."

Doug could tell from her voice that she was upset so he relaxed. "Kely, . . . is everything alright?"

Between sobs and sniffles she paused then barely whispered. "Doug, Katy died at 9:14."

Chapter Thirteen

A nearly inaudible moan came from near the bar. Both men's eyes expressed surprise, thinking that everyone there was already dead. They knew it could not be Mr. C since he still stared off into space.

Marc looked at Doug for guidance. His eyes grew wide, broadcasting sudden anxiety; he glanced at the shotgun.

Doug was on the phone with Kely but could not speak.

He shook his head at Marc then motioned him toward the broken bodies. Apparently someone was still alive and he should check it out.

Kely gained her composure.

The soft words about Katy's death crushed Doug's heart. They echoed endlessly as his awareness collapsed around him. He fought to deny the tears welling in both eyes. His pleasure at finding and killing Mr. C was ripped away from him. His willingness to fight any more was gone.

Overwhelming love of Catherine scratched and kicked at him as if to steal his very breath away. He fought for control of his body. It resisted as tears flowed. He hid them on his sleeve as though they had not occurred.

After prolonged silence Kely spoke. "You okay, Doug?"

He searched for a voice but none came.

"Are you there, Doug?"

He groaned softly to let her know he had heard.

"It's okay, Doug. You don't have to speak for a while

but let me tell you what happened.

"Everyone thought the repairs on her heart had worked okay but it failed causing a hemorrhage around 8:45.

"Internal bleeding was identified quickly by the monitors but it could not be stopped in time. She was rushed back into surgery but it was too late to save her life.

"The doctors were surprised by the bad turn of events. It was just something that happens, Doug. And, no one could really explain why."

Finally Doug was able to speak. "Did she wake up?"

"No. I wish she had. There was so much to be said. Are things worked out with Mr. C?"

"Yes."

"Is he going to leave us alone?"

"Yes."

"Did he hurt you any more?"

"Not really, just a few more bruises and scrapes; nothing really major."

"So tell me what happened?"

Doug hesitated. "I killed everybody in sight except for one guy. He's here now."

She gasped. "Is Mr. C dead?"

"Yes."

By the time Doug had ended his conversation, Marc had discovered that the third man was indeed alive. He dragged him away from the bar leaving a trail of blood. He had even removed his shirt exposing multiple wounds.

Doug's first action was to make sure the man did not carry a gun. He was clean, not even wearing a holster.

Three bullets had hit him squarely in the chest. One was low enough that it might have punctured his stomach. The entire front of the man was covered with blood.

Doug explored the man's badly injured chest. Marc found towels behind the bar and Doug used them to make pressure bandages just like a battlefield dressing.

The man had lost a lot of blood, was incoherent and able to make only an occasional moan. Marc wiped blood from his face and positioned his head on someone's folded jacket.

"You look like you know what you're doing."

"Yeah, I was discharged from the Army just before Desert Storm ended."

"Were you a Medic?"

"No, I was drafted into it when that Scud missile hit our barracks in Saudi. There were lots of dead and far more seriously wounded GI's than could be handled so everybody got involved in rescuing the survivors."

"What was your specialty?"

"Infantry and heavy weapons."

"Why'd you get out?"

"Another rug-rat came along and Lucy and I just couldn't live on what the Army paid me. With two kids Lucy couldn't make enough working part-time jobs to even pay the sitter so I bailed for more money!"

The wounded man's breathing now seemed regular. That was often an important sign. He still moaned occasionally but it looked to Doug like he might live. Doug adjusted one of the bandages making it tighter to stop the bleeding.

As they talked, Marc continued wiping blood from the man's chest and arms, then Doug saw it--the Eagle, Globe and Anchor, the emblem of the United States Marine Corps. *This man was a Jarhead too!*

Instantly Doug remembered sitting in front of his Quonset Hut back in bootcamp at the Marine Corps Recruit Depot in San Diego. The platoon was gathered around Corporal Ron Slater, holding one of his afternoon bull sessions. He usually talked more like a big brother than a Drill Instructor.

As the youngest of the Drill Instructors, he was Doug's favorite. His smoky-the-bear hat with its rigid brim and Marine Corps emblem captured and held the attention of most recruits. His barking of commands on the drill field became the standard for developing their own Marine voices.

This was when he answered questions about how to behave as Marines. The hazing of the prior months had wiped out most of their past attitudes and especially their relaxed civilian demeanor. This was where they learned new ones.

Of course his talks were another form of indoctrination. That was the Marine Corps' way of passing the torch to its young warriors. They knew that and each one wanted it to be exactly that way.

During that time of Doug's life being a Marine was the only thing that mattered to him. He wanted to succeed at it more than anything else in his life and he was certainly not the only one who felt that way.

Bootcamp was extremely competitive but at the same time, it was a group exercise in cooperation. It was one of the paradoxes in his early life and it stayed with him over the years. *Such a meaningful idea: Compete, yet cooperate!* It took him years to figure out what it all meant. It took still more years to finally make it work.

Slater planted seeds in their minds during those afternoon discussions and of course they provided him with very fertile soil. Many of Doug's deepest beliefs sprouted from those laid-back bullshit sessions. For Doug a special peace of mind resulted. He owed Ron Slater a lot.

That afternoon they talked about the image of being a Marine. What did it mean? Sure some Marines would be badass fighters in combat but most would not. Of course some Marines would be good street brawlers but most would not. The badass fighters and the good street brawlers were seldom the same people. The only reason he offered was that they were usually very different kinds of people.

Doug remembered Slater's words. "The Marine Corps is like few other places you'll ever go in life. Every Marine gets the same level of training. Everybody marches, shoots and learns personal discipline. What each one of you does with it is all that really matters.

"Some of you will excel, hopefully doing great and useful things. While others who try just as hard will achieve much less, maybe becoming complete failures. Remember that the trying is all that means anything.

"Some of you will win, others will lose. When you lose at anything, just do it a bit better the next time. That's all anyone can ever ask of you. The day may come when you will go into battle and maybe die. Marines train damn hard to reduce that possibility but in battle that's not always enough; that's what prayer is for, use it!

"When the enemy fires at you, his bullet ceases to have a brain. Lead destroys whatever it hits, killing the best, the brightest, the average and even the worst among you. Bullets just don't give a shit. They simply can't tell the difference.

"Being in battle is a lot like a turkey-shoot. You just never know when it's going to be you or the guy next to you so get used to it. You or some of your friends might die. Every day learn to live with it because that's your life now. That's what Marines are expected to do.

"If it happens then just look the fucker who shoots you straight in the face. Tell him you're ready to die because you're a Marine and be glad the Marines made you ready to face your own death with honor. If your chest is blown open, you'll probably die. You'd better kiss your ass goodbye with pride because that's all you've got left. The pride in being called a Marine.

"During the past fifteen weeks everyone of you, every last swinging dick, has worked his ass off and it was no small achievement. None of you have anything you didn't earn the hard way.

"Well, it's time for the payoff. In a week you'll be leaving bootcamp. You'll each have fresh haircuts and neatly pressed uniforms. Some of you will even get promoted.

"Downtown many young men look exactly like you except for their haircut but there's something else that sets you apart. Something they can never have that each of you will until the day you die."

His final words burned into Doug's brain.

"You are a member of the proudest, most dedicated, most capable military force in the world. Every Marine has achieved exactly the same as you have. The honor of being called a United States Marine until the day he is laid to rest."

Slater paused for a long time. Everyone felt restless with anticipation for what he would say next. "From this day forward every Marine is your brother!"

Through the years those words echoed in Doug's every behavior. He would treat this man with respect.

Doug stared blankly into Marc's face. Marc spoke but Doug did not hear the words.

Doug responded with his feelings. "We've got to get this guy to a hospital."

"We can't do that. Mr. Gallo said that they ask far too many questions. There's a special doctor we're suppose to call at times like this."

"What's his name?"

"I don't remember. Maybe there's something on Mario that'll tell us who to call."

Marc moved toward Mario and started rummaging in his pockets. He tossed Mario's things on the floor as he found and removed them.

The wounded man moved slightly and Doug raised his head with his arm. The man opened his eyes and stared at Doug as he tried to speak.

Doug cradled his head closer much like holding a baby. He could not understand the mumbling so he pulled the man's face closer. His ear touched the man's lips.

It was still impossible to understand what he tried to say but he was definitely trying to speak.

Doug called to Marc. "You finding anything there?"

"No, nothing, yet!"

"Keep looking. I'll find out what this guy wants to say."

Suddenly, Marc blurted. "Oh, shit!"

Doug looked toward him as Marc stood up and raised his hands. Doug turned toward the door to see what had stolen Marc's attention.

He gasped in surprise. Four men stood in the open doorway. Each held a pistol and they were all pointed at him.

Chapter Fourteen

A well-dressed man stepped through the line as the gunmen moved aside. Obviously, he was in charge.

He motioned toward the wounded man that Doug cradled. Another man emerged from behind the gunmen with a black medical bag. He stooped and began examining the man's wounds.

"What the hell has happened here?" He was a tall man, at least six foot two with dark, thick hair. He looked more like a Wall Street Banker than another mobster.

Doug answered. "Mr. C ran into some trouble."

"I can see that. Who are you?" He stepped closer. The gunmen followed behind him and surrounded Doug.

"I'm the guy who caused him all the trouble!"

"So you're that shooter from Atlanta he's been squawking about all week?"

"Not hardly. Is that the bullshit story he told you?"

The man raised his eyebrows with interest then spoke softly. "Do you have a better one?"

Without speaking the doctor injected a clear liquid into the wounded man's arm.

"Maybe, after I know who I'm telling it to."

The man straightened up and bowed slightly. He spoke in a formal voice. "I'm Bruno Sebastino and I don't like your wise cracks, Mister!"

Doug responded. "Okay. I'm the guy who spilled a drink on Mr. C in Las Vegas last weekend. That's how all of this shit got started."

He paused as if thinking then asked. "You did all this over a spilled drink?"

Doug pointed toward Mr. C's lifeless body near the bar. "I didn't try to do anything until that fat tub of shit tried several times to kill me."

"So you're saying that Fred started all of this?"

The doctor applied a blood pressure band to the man's arm and began listening for his pulse.

"Yes, I believe it was him who kept it going."

Bruno turned to Marc who was standing next to Mario's body with his hands raised in the air. "How do you fit into all of this?"

Marc answered calmly. "I worked for Mr. de Casale. He hired me two days ago."

"Did you see what happened here tonight?"

"Yes, sir. I did."

"Is this guy telling the truth?"

"I think so. That's the same story he told us when Mr. de Casale was still alive. It seemed to upset Mr. de Casale."

Bruno looked back at Doug. "So, Rambo, how'd you manage to pull this off?"

"It wasn't that hard. Mr. C's not very competent."

Bruno nodded. "So this is one of Fred's cover-ups. I told him years ago to cut out the games because I wouldn't tolerate them any longer. Looks like he got what he deserved."

He stepped closer and leaned toward the doctor. In a soft voice he said. "How's Jerry?"

The doctor spoke without hesitating. "He's lost a lot of blood but I think he's going to make it."

Then the doctor raised his eyes to Doug. "Did you stop the bleeding here son?"

"Yes."

"You did a good job with those towels."

The doctor stood up and looked Bruno straight in the eyes. He spoke like a dear old friend. "Bruno, you owe this man. He saved your boy's life!"

Bruno walked to the table and pulled a chair aside. He sat behind Doug but faced him. With a hand motion the gunmen stepped aside.

Bruno ordered another nearby gunman to get someone to come and clean up the mess. The man pulled out a cellular phone and placed a call as he walked toward the hallway.

Now the tone of Bruno's voice was friendlier. "What's your name?"

Doug turned, speaking directly to him. "Doug Carlson."

Bruno spoke like an executive, clear and concise. "Well, Mr. Carlson. We have a problem. Do you have any ideas how we might resolve it?"

"I think so. Mr. C's just made a contract for you to kill me, didn't he?"

"That's part of it. My son, Jerry, was here to finalize that contract. That's him you're holding."

Gently, Doug lowered Jerry's head back to the folded jacket. Doug moved toward Bruno.

"You're not going to carry out that contract, are you?"

"I have to. Somebody makes a contract; somebody carries it out. That's how it works."

At first Doug was surprised, then he wasn't. After all this person was a gangster. *What else should I expect?*

Bruno continued in a soft voice. "Here's the way I see it. You and Fred have a feud. He's got more muscle than you but you got smarts."

Doug nodded.

"Fred thinks he'll need some help so he buys it from me. Jerry gets in the way and you shoot him. What I can't figure out is why you then tried to save his life?"

"Wait a minute, I didn't shoot your son! Look around, everybody's hit with a .45 except for Jerry. Mr. C shot him while he was shooting at me."

Bruno waved his hand and two of the gunmen moved about inspecting the bodies. After conducting the inspection they both nodded in agreement.

"Okay so you didn't shoot Jerry. There's still the matter of the contract."

"It seems simple to me. Just let it go!"

"I can't do that. Once a contract's made, it must be carried out. It cannot be undone just because we become pen pals, that's the code."

"So, do you know for sure that they completed it."

"No but Jerry can tell us that when he's able."

Bruno spoke to the doctor. "Enrico, can he speak anytime soon?"

"I think so. I'll give him a stimulant; that should bring him around in a couple of minutes."

"Fine." Looking at Doug, Bruno said, waving his hand around the room. "After all this why would you even bother with trying to save Jerry?"

"I was only here to kill Mr. C, nobody else. He . . .."

Interrupting, Marc spoke. "Excuse me, sir, that's the truth. He didn't shoot me either. When we both first heard your son's moans, he took right over. Mostly I watched."

Bruno looked annoyed waiting for him to finish.

Then Doug completed what he had been saying. "I didn't

see him with a gun and he didn't try to kill me. When I discovered he was alive, I helped him as much as I could. No real reason, it was just the right thing to do."

Doug's mind jumped about for more of an answer. He remembered what he had told Catherine about the first man he had killed. In spite of how he had hoped to avoid it, he had killed too many people tonight.

It was like being in a war all over again. Painfully it hit him that the daily war on the streets of LA was no different than the war he had fought in the jungles of Vietnam.

Bruno inquired of Doug. "What if he'd also been shooting at you?"

"Then I would have killed him too!"

Nodding, Bruno pursed his lips. Looking around the room at all the bodies, he spoke sarcastically. "I also saw those two guys you clocked out near the front gate. How many other people just happened to get in your way?"

"More than I'd care to think about; that's not how I hoped it would be but . . . .."

"So you were only defending yourself?"

"Yes, sir, that's how I saw it."

He nodded again. "Are you the guy who was with Catherine Walker when she was shot yesterday?"

Doug was unsure what was on Bruno's mind but after hesitating he answered. "Yes, that was me."

"Interesting, isn't it? You know, how the media has reported her unfortunate situation."

"What do you mean?"

"Do you know she passed on earlier this evening?"

Doug felt tears in the edges of his eyes. He just nodded.

"She's become quite a local hero. Right now, there's ten thousand people gathered around Westside Hospital. It's blocked on all sides for five or more blocks. There's a candlelight gathering for her taking place right now, you know in her honor. She's a very popular well-loved woman."

"That's nice, she was very special to me too."

"Well, I don't exactly care for the part of her story involving the mob. What do you know about that?"

"Not much. The media put that together from their own sources using eyewitnesses and police reports. I don't think she ever said anything to them about it. I know that I certainly didn't."

Enrico interrupted saying that Jerry was now able to talk but only for a couple of minutes.

Bruno moved his chair closer and spoke to him. "How you feeling son?"

"Okay, Papa. This doesn't look too good, does it?"

Enrico was holding Jerry's hand. Bruno grabbed both of their hands. Gently he squeezed. "Ah, don't worry about that. Things'll be just fine."

Next he asked the question. "How'd it go with Fred?"

Jerry responded. "Not good, Papa. After a while he started backpedaling. He wouldn't pay more than 400. He even had the money in a bag under the table to further tempt me. He said if we didn't take the money he'd get those guys out of Seattle."

"So he didn't make the contract."

"No, Papa. The worm only tried to stiff us again."

Bruno raised his voice. "That sleaze bag, piece of shit! If he wasn't already dead, I'd do it myself."

"One more thing, Papa. Fred's the one who shot me."

"Okay son. You rest now."

Looking to Enrico, he asked. "Can he be moved?"

"I think so."

"Then take him home."

Immediately two of the gunmen put their guns away and picked up Jerry. They carried him out of the room with Enrico following closely behind.

Bruno stood and turned to Doug. "Well, Mr. Carlson. Looks like we don't have a problem after all."

"I'm sure glad to hear you say that, Mr. Sebastino."

"Look, let's start over here. What do you say?"

Doug agreed. "Okay, I'd like that".

"You saved my son's life. You call me Bruno, right?"

Doug did not want to be that friendly but it would be nice to stay on his good side.

So, he said. "You got it, . . . Bruno."

"What was your first name, again?" He asked.

"Doug."

"Doug, I owe you. Enrico is right. I owe you big time for saving my boy."

"No, you don't have to . . .."

"That's my only boy, Doug, and to show my thanks there will always be a place for you at my family's table. You're like family now!

"You have given a father the greatest gift of all. You've given me back my son and I won't forget it."

"Bruno, I appreciate what you're saying but . . ."

Again he interrupted Doug by raising his hand. "Stop. I won't have it. I simply won't allow you tell me no on a matter as important as this one."

Using his hands he motioned. "Look at me! I'm an old man. A man my age needs to have younger men around him. After dealing with this situation, you have proven yourself. I want you to be one of those men."

"I'm flattered, Bruno but I've got other priorities like putting my life back together for now."

"I understand. How are you, shall we say, financially?"

Doug was surprised that Bruno would ask such a personal question but he responded. "Not bad. I've got money in the bank and a few stock investments. Of course, Mr. C did torch my house and stole four thousand dollars from me in Las Vegas but I'm okay."

"Yeah, I remember about your house from the news." Bruno moved around the table and picked up the bag of money. He tossed it onto the table.

With a big smile he said. "In that case this probably belongs to you now."

"How do you figure?"

"Well, all Fred's property can easily be transferred back into the company. This money was intended for you, indirectly. That's how he planned to spend it but now he's dead. His organization's gone; the moneys accounted for. This was his personal property."

He pushed it across the table and said. "Understand?"

Doug reached for the bag, not wanting to argue. "Okay. It's my money. I'll take it." It felt heavy as he tossed it on the floor among the guns.

Bruno motioned to his men. They holstered their guns and left the room. Bruno followed them but stopped momentarily near the doorway and turned toward Doug.

"Remember, I always tend my obligations; they're a sacred duty to civilized men." Bruno extended his hand to Doug. They exchanged a friendly handshake.

Bruno turned and walked away.

Doug looked at Marc. "Do you believe that?"

Marc looked puzzled and did not speak.

Doug asked. "You have a car here?"

"Yes. It's parked out front."

Doug opened the moneybag so he could store the guns in it. He stared and thought how nice all that money looked. To make room for the guns, he removed several handfuls of cash and placed them on the table in front of Marc.

Doug pushed the stacks of bundled hundred dollar bills toward him. "This is for you, Marc. Can you stay out of trouble now and get a real job?"

Doug hoped the money would help him and Lucy stabilize their lives.

Marc grinned as he reached for the money. "You got it, buddy! It'll be nothing but the straight and narrow for me." He raised his hand like he was making another promise.

"Good."

Doug loaded the guns into the bag while Marc stuffed bundles of cash into the pockets of his jacket. When they were both ready to go, Doug smiled at Marc's happiness. They headed toward the door.

Doug spoke. "Let's get out of here, Mister Turner."

Chapter Fifteen

After Marc dropped him off at the hospital, he rushed upstairs to find Catherine. He shuffled clumsily through several groups of mourners before he reached the door.

A camera crew spotted him but he eluded them.

Kely waited in Catherine's room for him. She had assured him that no one would move the body until he arrived. The staff had taken away the medical instruments as well as the tubes, sensors and facial bandages. Except for bruises and minor scrapes, she looked like she was asleep.

Doug reached toward Catherine placing his left hand on her shoulder. His heart ached from a growing pain. Its beating echoed throughout his torso. He could not speak.

Doug just stood with tears running down his face looking at Catherine's body. Seeing her like that hit him hard.

Catherine was dead. She was gone. *FOREVER!*

He could not take his moist eyes off her lifeless face. She looked as beautiful in death as she had in life. He loved that woman and it took seeing her like this to finally make him feel it deep inside his heart.

He wished now that he had told her more often how much he loved her. *I should have done much more to let her know! A whole lot more, I should have married that woman. That's what I should have done. I should have married her. If only I hadn't waited.*

She deserved much more than this. She wanted a home

with a couple kids and a man devoted to her.

New tears welled in his eyes.

She would miss the joy of planning summer vacations, taking the kids to the doctor and to their first day of school, planning their birthday parties, meeting with their teachers. She could not sit with them during nights of childhood sickness. She would miss having grandchildren around her when she was old. None of that could happen now.

He sensed the fullness of her loss.

After a few minutes Kely moved closer and hugged him from behind. With her head softly against his back, he felt her arms encircle him and close in the front.

He raised his hand enclosing hers.

Doug heard her sobbing as pain gripped her heart too, the pain that only a broken heart can bring, the pain of losing a sister, her only sister, the pain of being alone. Doug knew that now she felt it all. He shared her pain.

Doug reached for the telephone on a nearby table and called Catherine's number. After two rings the machine answered. As the message began playing, he listened to her happy voice. Again tears flooded his eyes.

He pulled Kely closer so that she could share the precious moment. She gasped but held her cheek riveted to his. Their tears intermingled as they watched the woman they both had loved lying dead before them and heard her cheerful voice on the telephone.

After the beep Kely took the receiver and left a message that only could have been spoken by a dear, loving sister.

Doug noticed Rachel, one of Catherine's nurses, standing near the doorway wiping her eyes. Their gaze touched. She stared for another second then backed out of the room wiping her eyes again as she closed the door.

He and Kely both felt the loss but in the deeper human sense they would actually never be without her.

Kely hung up the telephone then stood leaning over a table with her back to Doug and sobbed quietly for a moment.

She straightened up and turned to Doug. "Since you were Katy's mate I think that makes you my brother. Now you're all the family I have left." She began to cry again.

Nodding, Doug placed an arm around her.

They held the embrace.

Their heads rested side by side. They squeezed each other hard as if it might make everything better. In just one day, both lives had been changed so dramatically.

Doug had always accepted this kind of uncertainty and knew it was normal but not with such a level of awareness.

Kely broke the hug first. She pulled back and went to her purse for a tissue. In a moment she turned to face Doug.

She spoke softly. "I've been thinking about Katy's headstone. What do you think of this?"

She handed him a piece of paper.

Reading it twice, Doug said. "That's nice, I like it. I think she would approve."

Sunday was a strange day for Doug. He and Kely spent several hours on the beach, listening to the surf, talking about Catherine and crying together.

On Monday, Doug went into the office for the first time in a week. Jessie, his boss, had heard about him and Catherine on the news so she had put him on vacation during the entire time.

She begged him to tell her the rest of the story behind the media reports. Doug started with a portion of the story but stopped when she began to cry.

It was interesting for him to see how another person responded to the events. He knew they were terrible but had no idea they were as bad as they actually were.

Later in the morning, Doug called Agent Townsen. He wanted Doug to come in for a debriefing but Doug refused. After Townsen finished shouting, Doug told him everything that he wanted the FBI to know, which included just about everything except Bruno, Marc and the money.

Townsen hinted that Doug was shadowed by one of his men the whole time he was inside Mr. C's estate but he refused to give any details.

Later that day while Doug was having lunch at an ocean front bistro, a man in a dark suit approached asking for Townsen's phone. At first Doug was startled but handed it over. After all, he had no more use for it.

The man simply said. "Thank you, Mr. Carlson." Then nodded, pursed his lips and spoke in a near whisper as he turned to walk away. "Good luck to you, sir."

Later that evening Doug counted the money, three hundred forty-six thousand dollars. Ninety percent of it was in bundles of crisp new hundred dollar bills. The rest, maybe thirty thousand, was tens and twenties.

Doug thought about how to get it all into a bank without creating suspicion. *What's the bank limits for cash deposits, five thousand, maybe ten?*

His insurance agent estimated the replacement cost of his house, three hundred ten thousand dollars. The property would be another hundred and fifty thousand if sold.

Doug spent the evening fantasizing about the money and how he might spend it. He wanted to stop working, to retire at his age, to buy a boat and sail the seven seas.

He noticed the clock at midnight. He went to bed still thinking about the bag of money.

Catherine's funeral was on Wednesday. It was intended to be small and uneventful but the media and the public had other ideas about it.

Doug could only guess at the number of mourners who attended. She was still being hailed as a heroine and the services were carried live on local radio and TV.

The overflow crowd filled the streets around the church and swelled the funeral procession to over five hundred cars. At the cemetery Doug estimated there were at least a thousand people. There were hundreds of graveside well wishers that neither he nor Kely recognized but he was certain that he had seen Jerry and Bruno's faces with several bodyguards among those in the crowd.

Afterwards when most had left and only a dozen close friends of Catherine mingled in small groups, Kely pulled him aside. "I booked that cruise we talked about last week."

Doug looked puzzled, causing her to respond immediately. "You know when Katy was in the hospital that first time. You said when this was all over we'd go on a cruise."

He remembered but was uncertain about doing it this early. "Oh, that. Do you really want to do it so soon?"

"Of course, that's what Katy wanted and I want to do it too, for her. We're the two who knew and loved her most in the whole world. I think now is the right time to do it. We each need the other's strength, understanding and compassion . . . and love . . . now more than ever.

"I think it's the best way for us to grieve and then to recover our love of life. We'll be able to pay tribute to Katy's love of life at the same time."

Kely put her arm on his. "Knowing Katy the way you do,

you know this is what she would have wanted."

Contemplating, Doug looked at his feet and kicked at a pebble with the toe of his shoe. He knew that Kely was right but his heart felt strangled. Of course he needed sunshine, warmth and the strength Kely was talking about.

He brushed the pebble one last time. He looked to Kely and smiled. "Okay, you're right. What's the schedule?"

"We leave Saturday morning at 8:20."

He nodded and took her hand as they walked away.

Pausing, he turned to take one last look at the headstone sitting to the side of the open grave. He read it.

CATHERINE ALICE WALKER
November 15, 1952--December 15, 1990
Katy loved life honestly. She lived it courageously.
She died doing both. Here lies a woman of the ages.

Doug moved into Catherine's house. He felt comfortable there. Being among her clothing, pictures and furniture made his loss feel less severe.

He stashed the moneybag and the guns in the attic hoping that they would be hard to find. He had no idea what he would do with them after the cruise.

His insurance agent offered to deposit the payoff check for his house as soon as it arrived in her office. On Friday morning Jessie located a building contractor who agreed to buy his property and rebuild the house for his family.

Doug thought about all the problems he had faced during the last two weeks. Now what he needed most was for things to be relaxed and to stay that way for a long time.

At 6:34 a.m. Saturday morning the taxi stood in front of

Kely's house. Both of them had completely filled the trunk and front seat with bags. Kely held the last one on her lap.

When they were ready to leave, she instructed the driver where to take them. "LA International Airport please."

Is Doug's fate with the Mob sealed?

In the second part of *The Dying Game Trilogy*, Doug rebuilds his life while working for Bruno Sebastino. He faces questions that could easily have been answered a year ago, but today too many things have changed. Most important of all, his life is no longer his own.

In *The Pact With Bruno* the reader is swept headlong into the wealthy personal lifestyle of a Mafia executive and his family. Doug's life becomes astonishingly intermingled with those of Bruno, Jerry and Kely. As relationships appear to strengthen, it becomes clear that all is not well. Shadows conceal a betrayal.

Without warning a new adversary appears who is much more powerful than Mr. C and Doug is at war again but for much different reasons. Can he handle this new challenge?

Look for this thriller in mid-1998.

Visit PCP's home page at http://www.pacificcoastpress.com/

David O'Neal was born on November 12th in French Camp, California shortly after World War II. He grew up in Tennessee, Florida and finally back in California. After high school he joined the United States Marine Corps where he received a Presidential Appointment to the US Naval Academy. Serving in the war in South Vietnam was his last duty assignment in the Marines.

He has education in City and Regional Planning with graduate studies in Cybernetic Systems. For over ten years he worked as a Business & Computer Systems Consultant. His first book was a technical reference manual published in 1992. *What Goes Around* is the first of three planned novels detailing the life challenges and personal choices of Doug Carlson.

Dave currently resides in the San Francisco Bay Area with his wife, Cheryl. He also has an adult daughter with two grandchildren living several hours away.